CoS1010

DISCARD

P9-DCP-074

A11903 734949

MP-17
1/95

DEMCO

RENEGADE MARSHAL

The year is 1875, when the railroads began their big push to conquer the heretofore unconquered West. The town is Pineville, a small place nestled underneath the Tooloon Mountains deep in the territory of Arizona. Newt Gobal, undisputed king of the nightriders, holds sway over the outlaws of the territory.

Then into town comes Orion Tibbs, convicted murderer and newly appointed U.S. Marshal. Recently an inmate of Yuma Territorial Prison, Tibbs has his work waiting for him as he takes over from Newt Gobal's self-appointed Roddy Ryan and finds every rider on the 'hoot-owl' circuit waiting for him and his gun . . .

Also available from Gunsmoke

RENEGADE MARSHAL

A. A. Baker

WESTERNS

Wes
BAK

First published 1969
by Avalon Books

This hardback edition 1991
by Chivers Press
by arrangement with
the author
in association with
Bobbe Siegel

ISBN 0 86220 975 7

British Library Cataloguing in Publication Data

Baker, A. A. (Albert Allen) *1910–*
  Renegade marshal.
  I. Title
  813.54 [F]

ISBN 0–86220–975–7

TO MY PLEASANT RE-TYPIST, MARCEIL

Printed and bound in Great Britain by
Redwood Press Limited, Melksham, Wiltshire

RENEGADE MARSHAL

CHAPTER ONE

Pineville, Arizona Territory, straddled an eroded mesa forty miles below Crater Pass. The town was basically a watering hole. Winter storms flowing over the nearby Tooloon Mountains dropped enough moisture to supply year-round water. Fissures in the buried stone provided subterranean channels that brought the water down to the free-flowing ponds. Massive buffalo herds had churned deep, swampy wallows into the earth, and somehow the water lasted through the dry season and, because of this, the town was built. Pineville stayed alive because it became the headquarters for the greasy buffalo hunters.

Close behind the maggoty skinners' wagons, miners had blundered into portions of the towering mountains and located copper and silver mines. As the buffalo died, cattle followed; longhorns grazed on grass fertilized by buffalo chips. The high mesa country held summer grass that also attracted sheepmen. The stockades below Pineville provided pens and lush green grass to take care of the lambing season.

Pineville was a shoddy town but one with a future. Baked by the summer heat and chilled by the winter freeze, it straddled the wealth of the mountains, with free access to the south via Crater Pass. The directors of the Territorial Shortline Railroad recognized this potential, and even now the tracks had climbed almost to the Pass.

Well below the Pass, where the ruts of the winding road straightened, Judge Leander Yontz drove toward town. When he kicked off the brake and flipped the whip the team broke into a brisk trot. Ahead, for the horses, was Omar Clay's livery stable. The judge leaned back and morosely surveyed the town. The few mercantile buildings, including Newt Gobal's pride, the Palace Hotel, lined Main Street. Stretching away like the spokes of a broken wheel, residential areas lay under a few scraggly pepper trees. Farther on, at the far end of Main Street, was Omar Clay's livery stable and corral. Beyond this was the Mexican quarter, built around Raphael's Cantina.

Soon—and this had led to Judge Yontz's trip to far-off Tucson—Pineville's isolation would be erased by the snaking rails of the new railroad. This future would depend on a number of intangibles. The railroad construction gang, led by Roger Allan, would have to get the rails over tricky Crater Pass. Some compromise would need to be reached between the cattlemen and Newt Gobal's nightriders. Yontz grimaced at the thought. The railroad could mean so much for this wild country, but the largest *if* was law enforcement. His trip to Tucson, an onerous deviation from his lengthy circuit, had been endured in the prospect of bringing effective law to Pineville and its surrounding miles.

A badge gave strength to a lawman, but only that

amount of authority the citizens were willing to release—and Pineville citizens had always been wary of surrendering any of their rights. The badge and guns of a local law officer were never very effective. Well— Yontz went on with his thinking while the horses hurried on—the next man to wear a lawman's badge in Pineville would have the support of the Territorial Governor. He would operate under Federal authority.

Leander Yontz, joggling along the flat stretch on the outskirts of Pineville, raised thin lips thoughtfully. The man he had chosen for the new marshal would never ask for help from the governor or, for that matter, any deity on earth or in hell.

Yontz pushed his dusty hat forward, eased his portly frame into a more restful position, and spoke to the rumps of the trotting horses. "Territorial law is a double-edged sword capped by a powder charge in the handle! It can cut with both edges and sometimes will blow up in the hand of the most chivalric user." He spat against the iron tire of the off-wheel, ran short fingers along the crease in his baggy woolen pants and fought off his doubts.

It had been done. He had the declaration. Pineville would soon have a new lawman by special decree of the Federal Governor. At least whatever legal hell broke loose after that would be sanctioned. Newt Gobal, the cattlemen headed by Garfield Piper, and the Roger Allan construction crew would be both protected and defended from each other. The slugs fired by the marshal would be legal slugs.

Yontz looked up as they entered town. Directly opposite, facing Main street with its windows broken
and oak-beamed door ajar, stood the Marshal's office.
He reined in and headed the team into the hitch rack
at Newt Gobal's hotel. Several inquisitive drinkers,
alerted by the jingle of harness, were already wan-
dering out onto the wide-beamed porch.

"It's the judge!" shouted a man who was dressed in
a weather-streaked Stetson, red suspenders stretching
over a vari-colored vest and a sagging pair of home-
spun pants. "Getting away from the circuit, Judge?"
he went on with a snickering leer. "How'd it all go
down at Tucson?"

"You'll see, Curley," Yontz parried, wasting time
until a crowd could assemble. "More important,
how'd it all go here in town?" The question brought
tight, secretive smiles from the bystanders and a
guffaw from Curley just as Newt Gobal sailed
through the crowd and answered Yontz's question.

"It's been peaceful, Judge," he said. "Whyn't you
stay away longer?"

Gobal fancied himself a handsome man and
dressed the part of the prosperous saloon owner. His
vest of green velour, pleated with red piping, was
studded with gold buttons and held together with a
watch chain of Zuni beads. The ornate vest covered a
pleated white silk shirt and a black leather string tie,
fastened with a Hopi silver clasp. His blue pants
were stuffed into immaculate yellow boots. Gobal sel-
dom wore the habitual gun belt but everyone present
knew that a four-shot Derringer nestled beneath the

wide waistband. Altogether, Newt Gobal was a restless block of a man who wore his power as boldly as any pirate. His aggressive energy dominated any gathering he joined. Here, at the wide door of his own hotel, his leadership was without question.

Judge Yontz, lifting his own eyes past Gobal's veined, pouty cheek, stared into the cynical, faded blue eyes and asked quietly, "How peaceful, Newt?"

"By number, Judge." He held up a long forefinger. "Number one—a gunslinger traveling through ambushed a citizen behind Clay's stable. Clear-cut case of robbery." Gobal pinched his lips together primly and popped his eyes wide. "But no need for you to fret, Judge."

"No?" The judge straightened his back while the laughter Gobal had solicited subsided.

⨍ "No need at all," Newt went on. "Pineville folks, they had themselves a hanging party. Even such a guilty jasper had himself a real trial. Then he was hung."

"That's the last lynching . . . !" began Yontz explosively.

Gobal interrupted. "Number two . . . There was a couple of Injun cuttings down by the old buffalo yards but . . ." He broke off, grimacing.

"What'd you do with the Indians," flared Yontz, "take their scalps?"

"Just run 'em off," Gobal said offhandedly, as though he condoned the fact that when Indians killed Indians it saved white men the trouble. He walked to the edge of the porch and stared into the steel-gray sky over Crater Pass, then turned back to the judge. "Where's all this law you been threatening us with? I don't see no cavalry following you. Seeing we're so important here lately, the governor should'a sent at least a troop of horse soldiers. With the railroad and all opening up Tooloon country, we need lots of law, don't we, Judge?"

Leander Yontz, descended from a long line of Maine sea captains, sputtered and finally lost his temper. "Tooloon country? Citizens? You're mostly scum, wharf rats and pirates! Panama pirates!"

Newt Gobal, pleased by his success in rousing the judge, was bland. "What about the law? We was promised Federal law when you hightailed it outa town to see the Territorial Governor."

Yontz gritted his teeth to calm himself before he answered. "The governor isn't going to send troops. They'll stay on the border." He smiled at Gobal's flushed face and went on confidently. "However, we're going to have our own U.S. Marshal." He began searching a voluminous coat pocket with a tense hand.

Newt Gobal shrugged and favored the gathering with a condescending smile. "We've had lawmen before, Judge."

The judge ignored the cryptic remark and leafed through his papers until he extracted a legal-sized document. His voice took on an acid edge as he replied. "You might have had lawmen before, Newt, but not one like you're going to get!" The buggy spring sagged under his weight when he stepped onto

the wide boards of the porch. Unrolling his proclamation, he pushed through the assembled hecklers.
They flowed in behind as he shoved the thick paper
under a loose clapboard and stepped back.

"The governor recognized," he stated sonorously,
with the same acid sharpness he used on the bench,
"that a railroad under construction in the Tooloon
Mountains must not be delayed by constant harass-
ment. Also, that cattlemen, sheepmen, miners and all
other citizens must be educated to live together in
peace. Further, the law-abiding citizens of the territory must be guaranteed protection and the lawbreakers must be caught and punished. The governor
weighed those items carefully and saw fit, in his great
wisdom, to appoint a U.S. Marshal. Said marshal to
be headquartered in Pineville." He pressed the
parchment flat until the fading afternoon sun lighted
the gold borders and the heavy red wax surrounding
the Federal Seal.

"Will you read it, Judge?" a fretful voice asked in
a defensive tone. "I'm too far back to see all that fine
print."

"Just the part," agreed Yontz, "below all the
whereases." He waited until the shifting feet and
snorts quieted.

Then, moving close to the wall for a better view of
Newt Gobal, began to read.

"'THEREFORE, BY THE AUTHORITY
VESTED IN ME BY THE CONGRESS OF THE
UNITED STATES, I PROCLAIM TO ALL RESI-

DENTS OF THE TERRITORY THAT ONE
ORION TIBBS IS HEREBY APPOINTED AS
UNITED STATES MARSHAL. HE SHALL BE
GRANTED SUCH AUTHORITY FOR ANY
AND ALL HONORABLE PURPOSES AS
THE AFOREMENTIONED JUDGE LEANDER
YONTZ SHALL SEE FIT TO ISSUE. ORION
TIBBS' GENERAL DUTIES SHALL BE THOSE
OF ANY TERRITORIAL MARSHAL AND HIS
ACTS AND BEHAVIOR SHALL BE THE SOLE
RESPONSIBILITY OF SAID JUDGE LEANDER
YONTZ. SIGNED AND DULY SEALED WITH
THE GREAT SEAL AS OF THIS DATE, AU-
GUST 30, 1875.' "

As he finished reading, Yontz flicked the document
with a snapping finger and added, "That's all. Marshal Orion Tibbs"—he repeated the name in a firm
even voice—"Marshal Orion Tibbs will arrive
shortly." He stepped back and watched the red blood
flood Newt Gobal's already florid face.

Slowly, Newt unhooked his thumbs from his vest
pockets and flailed the air with a chopping motion.
"You all hear that? Orion Tibbs, a U.S. Marshal.
The only Tibbs I ever heard of is that damned meat-
eating killer locked up in Territorial Prison!"

CHAPTER TWO

Seventy-five miles north of Pineville, Territorial Prison sat in open country. The walls and bastions were of quarried rock and surrounded the squat buildings housing the tiered cells. A dry wash, circling one-half of the grounds, served as a water storage area. Pools of brackish water had been dammed off and the prisoners hauled the water up into the prison by steep trails. It was a desolate place. Raw winds flung dust into the air and it seeped through the buildings and settled everywhere. The warden's office snuggled against the large gate, as though seeking respite from the elements. A scraggly patch of cactus served as a garden and lined the walkway.

Well beneath the ground level, a block of cells known as "The Hole" had been built for dangerous inmates. It was in the close confines of "The Hole" that Orion Tibbs squatted, listening to the firm steps of the guard approaching from the upper level.

He listened with some interest. It was too early for mealtime and the water *olla* had been filled yesterday. The person who now halted outside the cell door was disrupting the routine. A bolt was slipped and the small window pushed inward. Tibbs recognized the assistant warden, Carl Clopper. Clopper,

15

who had once served in a German prison, still carried his Prussian smartness into this far-off prison in Arizona territory.

Clopper carried a lantern and its light seeped through the cracks in the solid oak door panels. Tibbs traced the slivers of light with an inquisitive finger, shoved himself away from the sandstone wall and raised slowly to his feet. The shifting light sent yellow streamers over his naked ribs and lionlike mop of matted brown hair. The prisoner crept forward, sidling against the cold iron of the massive hinges, and crouched beneath the window. Now he could peer out and down through the cracks and be ready to leap when the door swung open. He smelled the fear that dripped with the sweat of his visitor; his hands formed claws and he gathered his muscles to leap.

"Tibbs?" Clopper's guttural voice quavered, then strengthened. "Get back away, you hear? You're to be taken out." His tone whined in a defensive plea. "The warden himself said you're to be taken out." The whine increased to mild hysteria. "You hear me, Tibbs? If you attack me, I will have to kill you!" The corridor hung with silence until Clopper shouted, "Answer, *dumkopf!*"

A thin grimace raised Orion Tibbs' lips but never reached the narrowed eyes. Finally he answered, and the words were like flint rubbed across steel. "Open up, Clopper. After thirty days in here, I'll even be glad to see you!"

Clopper lowered his voice to a wheedling whisper. "You be good, Tibbs? It's for your own benefit. To bring you to the warden's office are my orders. You are listening? Somebody important has come for you." Reassured by the silence, he raised the latch and pulled the bolt free. The door creaked as it opened outward. Holding the lantern extended and clutching a cocked revolver, Carl Clopper took one hurried step backward. "Maybe something good for you, Tibbs? Is two years and no visitors." His heavy jowls trembled but there was a trace of genuine concern in his light blue eyes. "You will see who it is, Tibbs?"

"I'll see who it is, Clopper," Tibbs stated with some relief. "I thought you were going to tell me the guard had died."

"The guard is all right. This is the truth. He is all right. And I told you, you're going to the warden's office. There is someone waiting for you."

"All right, don't chatter. Let's go on up and see what he wants."

After a brief halt at the prisoner's washing trough, Tibbs was outfitted with a clean cambric shirt and denim pants. A leg iron was fastened to one leg and his arms were securely held against his waist by a wide leather strap that fastened at his spine. Clopper, still with tiny worry wrinkles etched on his wide brow, ushered his prisoner across the yard and into the warden's office.

It was a large room, a showplace of burnished copper and calf leather. The sun, cooled by two feet of granite, filtered inside and glinted against the metal fixtures. White and black chairs with leather braces and slinged bottoms were a direct contrast against the multi-colored stained rattan mats serving as floor coverings. Indian relics, including rare Hopi spears and tassled squaw boots, occupied favored positions on the whitewashed walls. It was obvious that the man who had this office was proud of an historic past producing such mementos.

Warden Stephen Lowdnes, his back to the wall behind an eight-foot table serving as a desk, nodded as Clopper ushered Orion Tibbs into the room. The warden, with a greying mustache stiff with wax and a completely bald head, gave Tibbs a long, critical stare. With a hardening expression, the warden turned abruptly and addressed himself in a tone of sullen anger to Judge Leander Yontz.

"Judge Yontz, this is your prisoner and he's the meanest one we've ever handled in Territorial Prison. The governor's order to parole him in your custody requires me to doubt his sanity."

"Tibbs'?"

"Of course not," snorted the warden. "Tibbs is just a wild animal! It's you and the governor I doubt. Tibbs should be lined up against the wall and executed by rifle fire with dum-dum bullets. We've had a taste of his viciousness. A guard will be crippled for life because he tried to tame this killer. There's been no measure even mildly effective. The blacksnake, 'The Hole,' even Apache torture . . ." he threw up his hands in frustration, but caught his breath and raved on. "Tibbs is out of Mexico, a *pistolero*, a white man with a fast gun used to fighting bandits and Apaches. It's all killing and dying and makes no difference below the border. Tibbs lived most of his life down there and he should have stayed. We're not very civilized, God knows, but compared to Tibbs and his type . . ." This time the warden gave up and waited for Judge Yontz to comment.

The judge was cautious but blunt. "Well, he'll serve my purpose, Warden. I don't intend to tame him. He wouldn't be worth a damn." Yontz turned away from the warden and met Tibbs' eyes, adding, "I'm going to use Orion Tibbs to tame a town and a territory."

Warden Lowdnes rose abruptly as though he was in a hurry to have his office emptied. "Well, he's all yours, Judge. You've got him. We'll get the paperwork out of the way. Come along, Clopper." He motioned the assistant warden out of the room and closed the door with a snap that punctuated his impotent fury.

Orion Tibbs the outlaw, and Judge Leander Yontz, whose very existence was entwined with proper judicial procedures, faced each other in the weak light of the late afternoon. The room was filled with expectancy. To Tibbs, it was like an instant before the flogging whip snaked out to crack across his back. This had all happened so fast. He had been chained in an underground cell, breathing the close air, his mind blotted against the weary days and years of incarceration, knowing that while many tried, few escaped. Most died without a second chance to smell the fresh breath of freedom. To be sentenced to life and then to have that sentence lifted . . . the thought smoldered. This Judge Yontz had to be quite a man to swing a parole. Tibbs studied Yontz with some respect.

"I'd say you were a cut above the usual killer." Yontz moved out of the shadow, eyeing Tibbs. The shoddy prison clothing couldn't hide the litheness or the coiled muscles; the long legs and narrow hips that carried the deep chest easily; the lean neck and al- most massive head, the entire posture erect and proud. A trimming to calm the mass of brown hair, a close shave from a skillful barber, some regular cloth- ing, and Tibbs would appear as any other young, footloose Westerner. Most of them were alike, with little thought for tomorrow and no regrets for yester- day. They lived hard and died fast. Tibbs' reputa- tion was something a bit special; pure rawhide with just enough give, Yontz hoped, to carry the load Yontz had promised the Territorial Governor he could handle.

Yontz tried again. "Warden Lowdnes doesn't seem to like you, Tibbs."

"Is that a question or a statement?" Tibbs found his voice.

Yontz sprang forward, and grabbing a fistfull of cambric shirt jerked Tibbs forward. "Don't roust me, Tibbs!" He shook with anger, but instantly calmed and allowed his hand to drop to his side as he stepped back. "Just so we'll start out right, I've put my repu- tation on the line to arrange your parole. Now I wouldn't do such a fool thing without good reason, would I?"

"I guess not," Tibbs answered.

"I've got that reason. I need a lawman who can stand up to a freeze, a furnace, a flood, or a blizzard. He'll be needed to gun down gunslingers as much as he'll be needed to face them down. We've got a territory that needs taming. There's even a railroad coming in to open it up. There's cattle and sheep and mines. There are towns to be built so people can come and be content." His look was brooding and he was silent for a moment then went on.

"Right now, that territory is filled with hard men. Some as hard as you, Tibbs. Others—like Newt Gobal and Garfield Piper—are powerful and just as proud as they are powerful. They're the ones who'll buy your death, or even your gun." Yontz began nodding his head violently. "You'll see. You'll see."

"Is that where I come in?" began Tibbs easily

Yontz interrupted with a chuckle. "I haven't even asked you, have I? Well, let's make it official. You're to be paroled in my custody. Paroled, understand? One word from me and you're slapped right back in here, and from what I've seen of Warden Lowdnes, he'd like to have you back. In exchange for this freedom, you're to function as U.S. Marshal of Pineville and my circuit court area. D'you know that country very well?"

Tibbs nodded. "Lots of flat land with those Tooloon mountains snaking up right out of Mexico. The

Apaches could come north through canyons the
white man's never seen. And there're trails tromped
out by cattle rustlers even the Indians don't know
about." He smiled faintly. "Damned good country
for moving slow elk."

"I know, I know," Yontz broke in. "All I asked was
did you know the country. I was going to add that if
you act like the man I believe is hidden inside that
killer's facade, the governor will grant you a pardon."

"I accept," Tibbs answered quickly.

The judge held up a cautioning hand. "*Un momento,* Tibbs. Let me finish. I want you to understand that that pardon *may* be issued—posthu-
mously."

Orion Tibbs nodded. Judge Yontz stepped to the
door, disappeared, then finally returned with Warden Lowdnes.

"He's agreed, Warden," Yontz stated.

"I guessed he would." Lowdnes sounded grim.
"Clopper has the release waiting. We'll escort your
party . . ."

"No escort needed, Warden," objected Yontz. "I've
brought some clothing. If you can just furnish a
horse . . ."

"Hell, Judge!" stormed the warden. "You think
I'd mount him and let him ride outa here like he was
important? He'll ride outa here like any other prisoner—in the prison van." He gritted his teeth until
the mustache quivered. "Or, if you take him in the
buggy, *we* escort him off the prison grounds. Once
outside he's your responsibility so it don't mean a

damn to me, but I'll make one prediction." He drew in a full breath. "One hour after you take off those leg irons, he'll make a break. Even if he has to kill you, Judge, he'll make—or try—a break!"

Warden Lowdnes kept his word. The prison van, a black boxed-in spring wagon, was waiting in front of the prison office. Two armed guards, mounted on stout horses, escorted the van a full mile beyond the prison gates. The driver, while menacing guards watched, hammered the pins from Tibbs' leg irons. They watched until Yontz swung his buggy around and then, without a salute, rode off.

Tibbs changed clothing under the brittle sun. He stomped his new boots in the gritty dirt with a sense of satisfaction, pulled the new, flat-crowned Stetson over his eyes and waited for the judge to make the next move.

Without comment, Judge Yontz laid back the lap robe. A well-oiled gun belt, filled with gleaming brass cartridges, a Mexican embossed holster, and a blue steel, six-shot Colt gleamed against the robe. Finally the judge, in a sonorous voice, ordered. "Now, Orion Tibbs, raise your right hand and repeat after me." Slowly, Tibbs obeyed. At first he felt awkward, standing alone on the burnt ground facing the man on the buggy seat, but as the judge solemnly swore him in as a U.S. Marshal, Orion Tibbs relaxed and listened carefully. Yontz finished with, "So help you God," and passed the weapon down.

The new leather creaked and the blue barrel glinted as Tibbs strapped it around his narrow waist.

Tibbs drew once to test the weight. He spun the chamber and frowned up at Yontz. "You heard what Lowdnes said?" he asked slowly.

Yontz stared. Tibbs' lean right hand had become a claw, each tendon raised under the brown skin, blue veins etched down the long fingers.

"I heard Lowdnes," he rasped. "He said you'd kill me and run. That'd make you a walking dead man. Bounty hunters all over the West would make you a prime target. I told you once, I believe there's a real man concealed inside that reputation you've earned." The judge shrugged. "Anyway, when you play for big stakes you put up everything you've got."

"Those must be pretty big stakes." Tibbs slowly relaxed.

"Or, if you just run," broke in the judge, "you'd be an outlawed gunslinger. Hell, Tibbs, get into the buggy. It's a day and a night's ride into Pineville."

Orion Tibbs smiled thinly and climbed over the wheel. To his dying day he could never explain why he did. Maybe because Judge Yontz had made it sound so fine. A lawman with a territory to tame. A little, black-frocked man with enough courage to take on a land full of bandits certainly needed some help.

CHAPTER THREE

The hundred-mile ride from Yuma Territorial Prison to Pineville ended at dusk of the next day. Orion Tibbs, one booted foot on the mudguard, sat relaxed in the hooded buggy as the black team trotted down Pineville's main street. The sun, already blotted by the mountains behind Crater Pass, glowed against the tops of the buildings shading the street. Gobal's Palace, a full three stories with a false front, stood looming solidly over the marshal's squatty office. An evening breeze brought the smell of sage and tarweed in from the sandy valley. Sheep bawled from the stockade. The hitchracks were crowded and the tinkle of a piano mingled with the snorts of impatient horses. When the judge asked softly if it wasn't a kind of pleasant place to come home to, Tibbs had to nod in full agreement. A town not too big and not too small; mountains behind and lazy miles of flatland all around.

"There," Yontz pointed to the marshal's office. "Your headquarters."

It broke the spell. Orion Tibbs knew that he wasn't coming home; he was being brought in to kill. "There's a light, Judge . . ." He made it into a question. The light, to him, smelled of trouble. "Why should there be a light in the jail if the marshal didn't put it there?"

"I suspect Newt Gobal had it put there," grunted the judge. "Didn't I tell you about that, Marshal?" The word came out solid and strong. For the first time, Orion Tibbs realized this Judge Yontz was going to play it tough, all the way. He waited while the judge wheeled the buggy against the hotel porch, wrapped the reins around the whip socket, and sat glaring across at the lighted office. "Newt Gobal," he continued in a matter-of-fact way, "is the one I told you about, the one who owns most of the town. He swore in one of his fighting men, Roddy Ryan, as town constable. Newt had no more legal right to swear in a constable than Ryan has to occupy that marshal's office. Yet, normally, it's an effective approach. Gobal moves quick and he meets issues head on. Soon as he saw my notice that the governor had appointed a new U.S. Marshal, Newt acted. He tore down the proclamation, made a big holler about you being some kind of killer and . . ." Yontz paused and waited for an explosion from Tibbs.

"Go on, Judge," Orion Tibbs prodded calmly.

"Newt said Roddy Ryan was the only law Pineville was going to recognize. Plummer, the sheriff, hung by vigilantes in Alder Creek, used the same tactics. But I guess you know about that. No legal right—just downright brass." The judge came to a lame halt and climbed down from the buggy.

Orion Tibbs, face grim, stepped out on the street side, walked around the creaking vehicle and hooked a fist into the judge's lapels. The judge's face was a mixture of anxiety and determination, as though a decision had been made which could not be withdrawn. He let Tibbs have his say. "Don't roust *me,* Judge Leander Yontz! You want me to run off this Roddy Ryan? This fake constable appointed by Newt Gobal? You want him out of that marshal's office? Then, by God, you say so!"

Judge Yontz, face flushed with indignation, raised a hand to push Tibbs away, then hesitated. Tibbs was fiercely in earnest. "I *was* holding back," the judge admitted. "You want it on the line? Okay, then. I want you to run Roddy Ryan off. He'll fight you, but take him. By decree of the Territorial Governor, you're the U.S. Marshal and Roddy Ryan is occupying your place of business." Stolidly, he added, "There's only going to be one law around here and I want men like Gobal to know it!"

Drawing back a step, Tibbs slowly loosened his grip on the judge's coat and looked around. Three men, shifting their feet in nervous excitement on the hotel porch, were staring. The judge broke the silence. "What the hell are you staring at?" he bellowed. "Haven't you ever seen a judge manhandled before?" With a snort of disgust, he pressed past and entered the hotel.

One of the onlookers, obviously a bartender out for a breath of air, offered Tibbs some advice. "Go careful, friend. Roddy Ryan—when he was swore in —said he meant to stay on. Like Newt said, what right has that crazy judge to go bringin' in a con-

victed killer?" The speaker, realizing he'd spoken too
freely, made a weak smile that ended up a frightened
grimace and hurried after the judge.

Walking away, Tibbs circled the porch and studied the length of the street. The buildings, most of
them flimsy and unpainted, were joined by a rickety
boardwalk. Outbuildings, a barn or two, the water
tank and several clapboard stores, including one la-
beled "Haskins Mercantile Store," completed the im-
mediate business area. Behind, in the growing night
shadows, adobe huts were spaced by larger family
homes. To the south the street narrowed, and off the
entrance to Pineville an oncoming stage stirred up a
hazy plume of dust. Altogether, thought Orion
Tibbs, it was a dull and squalid place—a proper setting in which to die.

Swift strides carried him across the gravelly street.
When he reached the boardwalk, he sidled past several dark store fronts until he reached the corner of
the marshal's office. Behind the office, a narrow addi-
tion of thick adobe, with barred windows, squatted
in front of a small corral. Three horses were restive
and moved about in the gloom. Tibbs waited, judg-
ing the speed of the approaching stage. He could
hear the pebbles striking as the driver straightened
his leg on the foot brake to give the proper touch as
he swung the four horses close to the hotel entrance.
As Tibbs expected, the door to the marshal's office
snapped open.

A man in a tall hat, peaked above a narrow brim,
stepped out. A polished star bulged over a Durham

sack in the breast pocket. He wore a tied-down holster. The gun butt sagged several inches away from his thigh.

"Ryan!" Tibbs kept his voice low in a lethal hiss. "This is the Marshal. Drop your belt and stand still."

Roddy Ryan stiffened. Confused by the hiss that whispered out of the dark, he chanced a quick glance to locate the speaker. Tibbs, empty-handed, took one step away from the building and waited.

On the hotel porch men were gathering, trying to see over the top of the stage and waiting for the flame of gunfire. The stage driver, unaware, jovially shouted, "In on time, folks. Step down and enter Gobal's Palace. Finest eating and drinking place north of the border." His voice rose as he added, "Let the lady out first. The folks around Pineville are all waiting to see her." Peeling off a tassled glove, he slapped it against the hitching rail.

Inside the stage, Peggy Smith had edged over to the street side of the coach to watch the deadly tableau being played in front of the marshal's office. In the gloom, crowded in the seat corner, she wanted to cry out, but something held her in a tense grip. It was a living charade. Peggy drew the word into her mind as a person wills back dreams of an almost forgotten past. There were so many places, events and people she had put behind her. Words such as charade had little meaning any more. A dance hall entertainer had small need for fancy manners and even less for proper words, yet she was a spectator to a charade of death.

Both men were armed and crouched. Both men wore shiny badges. Peggy Smith wished she had the power to divert the approaching calamity but knew she could only sit quietly and watch it happen. The action followed her line of thought. In the next instant six-guns roared and it was over.

Bending a knee, the man at the doorway had whirled, his gun jerked from its holster. Peggy heard the metal slither against leather but the second gun had already spoken. The moment passed. Everything following was anti-climactic. Roddy Ryan's slug had skittered through the gravel. The stage horses were rearing at the noise of the twin explosions and were being gentled by the startled driver who shouted querulously, "What the hell . . . ? Someone could've told me there was a gunfight goin' on!"

"Nobody could shut you up long enough!" snapped a bystander. "That was Yontz's new U.S. Marshal and he just gunned down Roddy Ryan. We didn't even get to see it because you hadda park this danged top-heavy hulk so's nobody could see over it."

"Heard there was a new marshal up this way," offered the apologetic driver.

"There sure is," was the excited rejoinder. "And when the judge told Tibbs to go over there and clean out that marshal's office, he sure done just that!"

A voice in Peggy's ear brought her back to reality. "Sorry you had to see that, Miss Smith." Roger Allan spoke and she smiled at his controlled sympathy. He had boarded their stage at the construction camp near Crater Pass. She had learned he was a Boston man, a construction engineer now deeply involved in forcing stubborn rails over the Tooloon crags. His voice was taut and she knew he had been affected by the gunfight. The raw courage needed to face flaming guns had broken through his polished Eastern veneer. She nodded her appreciation for his compassion and then allowed strong, eager hands to help her from the stagecoach.

"Look who's come to Pineville!" squealed an onlooker.

"I been trying to tell you," shouted the driver, quickly recovering his aplomb. "An' she's fixin' to work right here in Gobal's Palace."

"Don't quarrel, boys!" Peggy pushed aside several hands and drew her tailored traveling duster snugly around her hips. "You can all buy me a drink." She made her shoulders tremble. "That was a little bit too exciting for me!" She arched a flirtatious glance around, avoided Roger Allan's musing face and marched grandly into the foyer.

Roger Allan, perplexed by Peggy's casual acceptance of the shoot-out, extracted a long cigar and, after chewing off the end, forgot to light it. It had been some months since he had left Boston. Conditions and especially moral values were so explosively different out here and men had such fierce loyalty for this wild land. The men were dangerous and so was the land. Death in man and animals was accepted, and not as punishment. Irritated, he threw the cigar into the dirt. Could he condemn Orion Tibbs' savage behavior? Roger Allan had to bring his railroad over the Tooloon to prove he was an engineer, just as Tibbs had effectively proved he was a lawman. Judge Yontz had promised to bring law into the Pineville country. That law had been slow in coming but this night Yontz had begun payment on his promises. Roger Allan mounted the hotel stairs and turned to look back once more. The lights in the marshal's office dimmed, then blacked out.

Inside the barroom, Judge Yontz and Newt Gobal were the center of an eager group. The lighted chandeliers dripped winking light, which reflected the dozen liquid shades contained in the bottles on the back bar. Peggy Smith was being escorted up the broad stairs by one of the other girls. A porter followed with a heavy carpetbag and a leather hatbox. When she reached the top, she turned to smile down on those below.

Roger Allan joined the men at the bar. He propped an elbow on the flat walnut surface, hooked his bootheel on the rail and listened to Newt open a harsh denunciation of Tibbs' behavior.

"It wasn't right at all, Judge! Roddy was there doing a job. What right have you or that Tibbs got, telling him to get outa that office?"

"Tibbs is the legal lawman!" snapped Yontz. "You had no legal right to make Roddy Ryan a constable. Tibbs was appointed by the Territorial Governor."

The calm assuredness of the judge was getting under Gobal's skin. "Territorial Governor!" he blazed. "We got that running outa our ears. Who made this country? The governor? No! We took it away from the Apaches and the rest of the horse Indians. We suffered through its growing pains. Then this Territorial Governor is appointed outa Washington." Newt Gobal whirled around to point a shaking finger at Roger Allan. "Just like *him*. Hired out of Boston to ruin us with a damned railroad. That's who's telling us now, a governor and a dude! Where was they when the Indians was overrunning every tent we hoisted?" He spun back to Yontz. "And you —you go on down to Tucson and spread a lot of bull!" His attack grew more vitriolic. "You make out us folks is against law and order; that we're a nest of lawbreakers; that we rustle cattle and hunt scalps for bounty. Even that we hold up stagecoaches." Newt raised his arms in mock horror. "So what does your Territorial Governor do? To control such a wild bunch—which *he* believes is running around out here—he goes crazy an appoints a *convicted murderer* as a U.S. Marshal! Right out of Territorial Prison. And the first day this marshal steps into Pineville, what's he do? He guns down the only law we got!"

"And all that is riding right on your back, Newt," stated Judge Yontz flatly. "If Ryan's dead, you engineered his killing."

"Murder—not killing—murder!" Newt shouted.

The judge held up a hand to quiet the explosive accusation from the hotel owner. He spoke in measured tones. "I put that notice up. I explained it was official. And what'd *you* do? Right away you pinned a constable's badge on your gunman and tried to make him the law enforcer. Right then you as good as signed his death warrant. You knew I was going to Yuma to bring Orion Tibbs back here. Everyone in this place knows Orion Tibbs can outgun the best man that ever stood up to him. I'm just wondering how many more of your gunslingers he'll have to kill before you learn!"

"Us—learn?" Newt Gobal swelled like a puff adder facing a bulldog and rasped, "It's going to be you and Tibbs got the learning to do." With effort, he calmed and began moving out of the tight circle. "But right now I got me a place to operate. There's the new girl . . ." He grinned easily and raised his eyes toward the top of the stairs but couldn't leave without a last threat. "Now, you hear me, Judge, and pass it onto your renegade marshal. This is a mighty big territory. My advice to you both is—walk easy." With this last thrust Newt shouldered past the judge and moved up the stairway.

Judge Yontz, boiling with anger, shouted, "*Renegade* marshal? Hell, Newt Gobal, you're the best example of a renegade I've ever seen!"

Newt, one foot raised to take another step, paused. His broad back hunched and the muscles bunched as he reached for his pocket Derringer; then he halted the move and turned with deliberate coolness. The onlookers hushed and edged to move away from the judge. Yontz stood his ground, expecting Newt to pull his gun but resolved to take it full on.

The hush was broken as a man clattered through the street door, pushed to the bar and importantly announced, "We hauled Roddy over to the Doc's.

There's a hole in his shoulder bigger'n a pick handle. The Doc won't say if Roddy's goin' to live." The man chuckled as he poured himself a stiff drink. "Old Doc Saber says Roddy was born to hang."

Completing his turn, Newt Gobal snarled, "A damned good thing for you, Judge." He smiled sourly. "Maybe that murdering lawman ain't the man he used to be? Them prison cells sometimes give a fella the shakes." Satisfied that he'd made a point, Newt continued up the stairway.

Judge Yontz, feeling a bit dismayed that he had opened an avenue of personal animosity, and a bit shaky now that the danger had passed, walked to the door. Roger Allan followed and they left together. Outside, the judge took the engineer by the elbow and walked him across the street to the marshal's office. Roger Allan, perturbed by the scent of danger, shifted his feet while Yontz knocked on the door, and wished the full moon would flood in. The town was hemmed by a half-light and it was terribly gloomy. Earthquake weather or a lightning storm affected him just as had the recent startling events. He could still smell the sharpness of burnt wadding and gunpowder.

The door swung open. Orion Tibbs' voice was vibrant in the warm interior. "Come on in, Judge." A lean hand turned up the lamp.

The room was small. Two long steps would cross it and five would bring a man up against the wall at the far end. An iron stove, propped on four stones, held a bubbling coffee pot. The rifle rack, empty now, with lock and chain dangling, stood next to the slit window. Overhead, the log cross-beams, laced with willow sticks, dripped spider webs.

Roger Allan stared. This was his first good look at the marshal. Wide eyes were deepset in the lionlike head. The eyes were narrow and sleepy now, like a torpid wolf. The lithe frame was at ease as the judge began introductions and Tibbs offered a steady hand. Allan noted the powder burns pitting the thumb knuckle.

"I told you about Allan's railroad, Orion," the judge began as he found a chair. He raised his coat-tails and spread his chunky legs out in complete relaxation. "You'll see a lot of each other. He rode in on the stage and saw your performance."

Tibbs nodded without speaking.

Roger Allan finally broke the silence. "I guess you did what you had to do?"

The marshal grimaced. "Ryan didn't have to draw."

"You really believe that, Marshal?"

Judge Yontz tensed and cocked his head at the sharpness of Allan's question. Orion Tibbs waited until the engineer found a seat before he replied. "Let's say that Roddy Ryan had to draw because— well, because he was a man. If he'd chucked his gunbelt, he'd have been called yellow."

Roger Allan understood. "How did you know Ryan would draw? Couldn't he have waited and shot you in the back, later on?"

Tibbs grunted and smiled as he asked, "The judge said you're building a railroad through the Tooloons? That's pretty tricky, building a railroad. Surveys, grading, handling crews?"

"I get it." Roger Allan smiled away his resentment. "Extracting a lethal weapon from a holster is a competition. Split-second perfection can be gained with a reasonable amount of practice. The difference between living and dying, once that gun is moved, apparently rests in the judgment and courage required to continuously compete and still stay alive?"

"Pretty close," Tibbs said.

"I'm building a railroad and that's pretty technical in itself. We're approaching Crater Pass with a track and have progressed a full quarter-mile into the tunnel. The graders and the rail-layers are doing well . . ."

"It's like fishing your watch out of a barrel of rattlesnakes," interrupted Judge Yontz. "The ranchers want it in one place and the miners want it in another. And then we got this outlaw element." His next words were a growl. "*They* don't want the railroad—period. Newt Gobal is behind that and I know it!" He glared at the two men and his voice rose. "That's why you two have to get along. That railroad has got to be built, and this is something you'd both better believe—it's going to take both of you to build it." He rose suddenly, nodded to both men, and walked out.

"The judge is a good man," offered Roger Allan lamely.

Orion Tibbs nodded in solemn agreement. Before the silence could flow in again, Allan offered a taciturn goodnight and followed the judge.

CHAPTER FOUR

The day following the shooting at the marshal's office ushered in some typically fall weather. The sky was pure steel. A glowering cloud bank, gathering overnight above the mountains, portended an early cold snap. The wind was blowing tiny granules from the sun-beaten ground and flailing them through the Pineville streets.

Orion Tibbs spent the day getting settled. Under the glowering eyes of Newt Gobal, he moved into the hotel. His room faced onto a narrow balcony with a steep stairway leading down to the alley behind the hotel. A ladder nailed to the clapboards led to the flat roof and his single-room window faced out on Center Street. He located the hotel swamper and paid him to swab out the marshal's office, then walked around to the general store.

In Haskins' cluttered mercantile store, he faced an unsmiling clerk and charged two double-barreled shotguns and a used Henry rifle to Judge Yontz' account.

Four blocks down, he located Omar Clay's blacksmith shop and arranged for that dour smithy to lop twelve inches off each shotgun barrel and to drop-forge ten pounds of quarter-inch pellets. The blacksmith shop fronted a livery stable, and when Orion inquired about horses, the sullen smithy became a gabby horse-trader.

It was cool behind the livery stable; a quiet copse out of the wind, where the marshal and the smithy enjoyed the afternoon putting spirited horses through their paces. As the afternoon wore away, Omar's clever improvising diminished and he trotted out a rust colored animal named "Mick." Noting the Morgan head, powerful shoulders and stocky legs, Tibbs bought the horse.

"That's quite a choice, Marshal." Omar Clay was aglow with admiration. "That's the sort of animal I like to sell. The one in a million. More than a beast of burden; a real friend, trained to stand without rein." He winked. "And to stand up to both barrels right in his ear without shying. Mick was a cavalry mount. He's used to the long trail on short rations. Just give Mick a little of the plug and he'll be your friend for life."

Orion held up a hand to calm the enthralled liveryman and commented, "He could be deaf?"

"No such a thing! You bring Mick back any time. I'll be glad to buy him right back."

"Same price?"

"If'n he's in the same shape," boomed Omar and held out a roughened hand. "Horsetrade?"

"Horsetrade, Mr. Clay." Orion rose to leave. It had been a relaxing afternoon, with the warm sun bouncing off the rough boards of the stable and the rich, humus smell of the corral and the horses. The brutal years at Territorial Prison would fade, but Omar

Clay's next words were a prediction of rough times to come before their fading.

"There's some . . ." Omar broke off, looked over his shoulder and lowered his voice. "There's some who don't want no law at all and ain't goin' to extend you no welcome, Marshal. Maybe Judge Yontz tipped you off there's somethin' big goin' on? I don't just mean about the railroad, either. This something is bigger even than the Territorial Shortline Railroad. Pineville—and every acre north of the border —is just one big sore bein' rubbed against a poisoned post. This country's got to have that railroad to be settled. Them who fight it has got somethin' in mind and that's not good for everybody."

"Someone like Newt Gobal?" Tibbs asked.

Omar Clay nodded. "That man don't want no law and he don't want no railroad. That make sense? And nobody asked him to make Roddy Ryan constable. No, sir. Newt put him in just to show up Yontz. Exceptin'," he grinned respectfully, "Yontz come out top dog cause you was the best man with a gun. Like that French fightin' . . ." He hesitated, seeking a word.

"Dueling?" offered Orion.

"That's just what them two was doing—dueling. Newt was using Roddy and the judge was using you. Was you killed, Newt would'a been the winner." He rubbed his head. "Don't make sense. Killin' a U.S. Marshal won't stop no railroad. When did one man's death ever stop progress? Newt Gobal's a saloon owner and he should *want* Pineville to be a railroad

stop. It takes people to ship out cattle, load out copper ore, and move sheep. The more folks, the more
money, and who don't like a bit of high living?" He
broke off with a plaintive thought as Orion moved
toward the corral. "I guess you and the judge know
what's goin' on?"

Tibbs answered soberly. "The judge must have
good reasons for wanting a marshal, Mr. Clay."

"I know. I talk too much," muttered Omar Clay.
"You come by to have me make a couple of shotgun
cannons and to buy yourself a horse. I'll just throw a
lead rope onto Mick and let you get along."

Exhausting its last glow against the cloud bank,
the sun had gone down as Orion Tibbs led his horse
up the alley. The alley was narrow and passed behind
the buildings fronting Main Street and the backyards
of the residential area. Lamps in the houses were
lighted and supper odors floated from the open door-
ways. Rocking chairs creaked and cigars glowed as
men rocked and waited for their supper. Tibbs was
conscious of reflective stares from the shadows as he
led Mick along.

Omar Clay had been prying. What did he expect
from a man who had arrived only the night before? If
Newt had some objection to the railroad that was his
own business. The judge was conducting a running
feud with Newt Gobal; that was certain. Orion chuckled and scratched Mick between the ears. Right
now he didn't particularly care what Judge Yontz or
Newt Gobal were promoting. Mick snorted and
Orion addressed the horse. "Don't ever tell, Mick,

but in a few days, you'll be a helluva long way south of Pineville. We'll be in the land of the jacaranda blossoms where the red pepper trees make such wonderful shade for the siesta." He patted Mick's neck and grinned. "How'd you like to own your own cornfield and a peon just to brush the falling blossoms out of your mane?" Orion slapped the muscled neck once more and added jauntily, "But first the *dinero,* Mick. *Mas dinero, sabe ud.*"

Intending to stop again at Haskins' store to pick up a saddle and bridle, he crossed the alley when he reached the back of the hotel. The tripping sound of a woman's heels floated down from the balcony. He looked up and saw Peggy Smith. She wore a red gown, a heavy silver necklace, and a comb with gleaming pearls in her shining hair. She had halted, facing away from Orion and called softly, "Judge? Judge, this is Peggy."

The judge, wearing the familiar frock coat and short-brimmed hat, eased out of a doorway. With careful steps he sauntered to her side. Making a hushing motion, he took her elbow and steered her to the doorway of his room. At the doorway he hesitated, then turned back to lean over the balcony. "Marshal?" His voice held no embarrassment but did seem a bit sharp. "I see you have a horse. Tomorrow we're riding out to Crater Pass. You'll get a look at the country and Roger Allan will have a chance to tell you all his troubles."

Orion nodded and dropped Mick's lead rope over a hitching post. "Tibbs?" It was Judge Yontz again.

This time his voice was overly nonchalant and Orion guessed that the judge might be blushing in the dark. "Let's not leave too early." He nodded his head toward the door where Peggy had disappeared. "Understand, Tibbs?"

Orion carried his gear from Haskins' store across to the marshal's office. The swamper had left a pot of coffee to steam on the stove. Tibbs drank a cup, rifled through a stack of dusty wanted posters, inspected the double cell in the back and finally, completely at loose ends, wandered back to the hotel. He stepped through the batwings to the bar.

It was a large room with a small dais raised a foot higher than the floor, obviously a small stage for entertainment. The usual nude painting hung behind the serpentine bar. Swinging lamps adorned with droplets of orange crystal reflected against the red and gold French wallpaper. It was a plush room and Orion felt a bit startled as he ordered a drink and turned to face the room.

Five men at the poker table were concentrating on the fingers of the dealing houseman. To the left, next to draped windows, a piano player wearing yellow garters caressed the keys. Drinkers, lining the bar and seated around the room, were heavily armed. Several women in the usual short and flouncy dresses promenaded among the tables.

"So you're that U.S. Marshal?" The low, teasing question caused him to turn. Peggy Smith, still in the red gown and silver jewelry, had moved alongside. Her lips were painted and her eyes were very large.

Her hand was warm on his forearm and he felt her tremble, yet there was no shadow of fear on her mobile face—just the hint of amusement in her words. "Would you like to buy me a drink, Marshal?"

"You can get your damned drinks from Yontz!" The retort startled the men in the room. Quick glances were thrown his way and a few chuckles raised in lean throats, then broke off short as they met Orion's stormy eyes. Peggy, shrugging in resignation, moved off. Orion, wishing he could recall the lashing words, gulped his drink and stalked out. As he climbed the stairway, amusement seeped through his rancor. At least Judge Yontz should be ready to leave early in the morning.

The judge came down with Roger Allan as Orion Tibbs was finishing his breakfast. Allan, in a pair of whipcord breeches, laced boots and a corduroy coat, nodded to Tibbs and slid into a seat. Judge Yontz threw an ankle-length duster over a chair and greeted Tibbs gruffly.

"Allan will join us. We'll inspect the Crater Pass tunnel. I'll leave you there and drive on east to Tonalea Wells. I should have four days on the circuit." He avoided any mention of the gunfight and they finished breakfast in silence.

Out in the street, Yontz mounted the buggy and made room for Allan. "You bring a horse, Tibbs. Once we look over the tunnel, you'd better ride on over to Rail Head for a look-see."

"What's over there?" Tibbs asked.

Yontz and Allan exchanged glances before Yontz answered him quietly. "Nothing—yet . . ."

"It's the alternate route," Roger Allan hurried to elaborate. "It circles the Tooloons to the south." He went on to recite roadbed cost, the savings on flatland track-laying and noted also that all towns would be bypassed. He admitted gloomily that the railroad would be strictly a line for loading cattle out for Eastern markets.

"Not even a town?" Orion questioned.

"Not yet," snapped Yontz. "It's where the cattlemen want the railroad to terminate. They've already got their city grid map laid out and a name for it— Rail Head. They'll begin building holding pens in the spring."

Omar Clay stood on the hotel porch sucking a toothpick. The blacksmith's face was solemn and pinched together, like he'd swallowed a bitter pill. He shoved both hands into his deep denim pockets before greeting Orion Tibbs. "You hear about Roddy Ryan, Marshal?"

Leaning down to take the slack out of Mick's cinch, Orion shook his head and waited for the bad news. The smithy spoke with needle sharpness. "Roddy died last night."

"So . . . ?" Orion straightened to mount.

"Roddy had plenty friends. You best watch out." Omar moved off the porch.

"I'll do that," Orion stated flatly and nodded his thanks. The real trouble was beginning to build up.

He had sensed the explosive restraint last night in the barroom. Newt Gobal would move now that Ryan was dead, and if Orion's judgment was right, Newt Gobal's revenge would come from some unusual angle. The slugs from a bushwhacker's rifle would have to let the territory know that Newt was still in control. When Judge Yontz's U.S. Marshal died, Orion grimly reflected, they would be sure to find Newt Gobal's coup stick nearby.

Yontz's buggy wheels sparkled in the morning sun as Orion settled himself in the creaking new saddle and gave Mick a playful touch of spur. Offended, Mick reared once and then galloped after the disappearing buggy.

CHAPTER FIVE

The sun had passed the zenith when they reached the railroad camp at Crater Pass. The pass, with entrance and exit as handle and spout, was shaped like a gravy tureen. The space between was a rounded pocket valley, guarded by black cliffs which caught sunlight in a glassy reflection. In some long-past eon, a volcano had erupted. The fire had died and the cone had hardened. A lava plug had broken through the wall crevices. More eons passed until erosion crumbled the cone and the remaining valley became Crater Pass. The railroad crew was blasting its tunnel through the crater rim.

"Looks like you're on the last leg." Yontz had reined in and studied the tunnel entrance.

"Soon as the timbering is completed," Roger Allan answered, "we'll lay out the roadbed on switchbacks —a fast three per cent grade right into Pineville." Perturbed, he shook his head. "We're going in on tiptoe, using very small charges. A tiny miscalculation— one overshoot—and we'll lose the tunnel. If that happens, we've built a railroad up into the Tooloons for nothing."

"Who laid out the route?" Orion asked quietly.

"I did," Roger Allan answered fretfully. "We had a survey crew in the Tooloons for over a year. I

47

warned the directors, and Wolfstein himself, against trying this route. Now we're in the crucial stage. We've spent too much to back out." He paused to study Orion resentfully. "If there's any more trouble . . ." he shook his head resignedly.

"Trouble?" Judge Yontz broke in heatedly, almost as though Orion Tibbs should accept some of the blame. "There's been sabotage and the work train was derailed twice, deliberately. Culverts were blasted out on Seven Mile Grade. Payrolls held up in the Tucson bank until they could be sneaked past the road bandits."

"This is our most pressing problem," admitted Roger Allan. "The road gangs haven't been paid for six weeks." He shook his head with dejection as he turned to the judge. "Your plan had better work. Wells Fargo has the money coming through on the next stage." He halted, stilled by a glower from Yontz.

Orion tightened his jaw. So—the judge was holding back again. Visit Rail Head, hell! He had been brought along to protect a payroll shipment, and worse still—kept in the dark until Allan let it slip. Gunning down Roddy Ryan had just been a gunfight to the cautious judge. Was he putting his marshal on the trail again? Orion turned away. For a few minutes he had been sympathetic to Roger Allan's problem, and was about to show him the old Mocassin Trail—a high road known to the Apaches and Spanish padres—which bisected the Tooloons by following high ridge country. The Trail had grades

easy enough for wagons and the huge loads pushed
northward by Indian slaves. More recently, it was a
perfect escape route for the "hoot-owl" riders. Now,
all he wanted was to get on over the ridge and meet
that payroll-carrying stage.

The judge, sensing his error, boomed heartily.
"You'll make it over the pass, Roger. I'll leave you
now and get on to Tonalea Wells. Whyn't you show
the marshal around?"

"Never mind," Orion refused flatly. "I've seen railroad camps before. I'll just jog on over the ridge and
meet the stage like a marshal's supposed to do."
Without further comment from the worried Judge
Yontz, Orion slapped Mick on the rump and trotted
off.

Two hours of easy riding took him through the
pass and well down through the timber line of the
southern slope. The solid rock had given way to tamarack crowded in among massive boulders. Here the
forest area was a mass of pine, spaced by creeping undergrowth struggling out of shaded ravines. Wild gra-
pevines, laced by crisp green ferns, crawled over de-
cayed snags. The road was merely a pair of staggered
ruts avoiding the canyons by staying high on the hog-
backs.

Orion's resentment had been replaced by a growing sense of freedom. Out there, in the hazy south,
lay Mexico. The Apaches had raided and swept back
across the border through these rugged mountains.
Down below, the escape trail circled through the
piles of bare rock known as the Chiricahua and the

Sierra Madres. This time, Orion reflected soberly, he wanted no part of selling his gun. He had, since leaving Territorial Prison, intended to stay on with Yontz until the opportunity to make a stake presented itself. Perhaps the Wells Fargo box might just be that stake. To hell with Yontz's big dream about the railroad and settled land, where law would replace the hot justice of an exploding cartridge.

The sound of whiplashed horses crossing a corduroy bridge caught Orion's attention. The wild hoorah of an excited stage driver was half swallowed by the walls of a small cut leading onto the bridge.

A shotgun blast, followed by the rapid explosions of a Colt, crashed through the trees. A woman was screaming as Orion sped forward. The stage was rolling across the split beams of the bridge, a dying driver lashing feebly with his whip. A masked rider had edged his horse up against the stage box and was dragging the Wells Fargo box from under the driver's seat. The man tugged frantically to lift the box onto his saddle. He succeeded—then, whirling his horse, disappeared into the heavy brush. The woman screamed again. The driver was flung aside as the stage tipped, off-wheels spinning in mid-air. The stage horses, harness tangled with the tongue, reared and fought against the drag of the jouncing stage.

Orion had reached the bridge. The stage was rocking dangerously as the horses plunged. The woman still screamed. He dismounted and scrambled into the melee of straining animals. He was able to locate the trace snaps and jerk the pin free. The twisting wagon tongue, free of the animals, dug into the peeled logs. The horses circled, tangled in the trace chains, then fought their way back onto the road.

The desperate few moments passed and the animals were calming. The stage creaked as it balanced on the edge of the peeled logs serving as a bridge over the deep ravine. The shifting weight of the woman passenger could send it over the rim.

"Stay still!" Orion shouted and she obeyed instantly. With an uneasy grimace of fear and indignation, she gripped the doorpost and froze. In seconds, Orion loosed his lariat and had a loop over the jutting brake handle. He urged Mick around, and with rope dallied on the saddlehorn took up the slack, and the stage slowly straightened and dropped firmly to the bridge. Dismounted, Orion reached up and tugged the door open. The woman, plump and fiftyish, placed grateful hands on his shoulders and he lifted her down. She stood for a few seconds, trembling and clinging to Orion.

"Easy, lady, easy." He helped her over to the bank and gently sat her down. Nervously, she worried with her hair, extracting a long sharp hatpin and clamping it between her teeth while she straighted her wide-brimmed hat.

"The holdup men . . ." she chattered past the pin.

"He's gone," Orion began but she quickly interrupted.

"I said there were *men*—two of them." Her eyes fell on the body sprawled across the bridge timbers. One look convinced her the stage driver was dead and she began to sob. Quaking noises separated her explanation but she went bravely on. "They—rode up about a hundred yards back and ordered the driver to stop. The guard fought but they shot him down. Then they rode alongside the stage, firing on the driver. They—they killed him and . . ." her voice broke on a wail of pity and horror. "In—in another minute we'd have gone off that bridge."

Orion uneasily watched tears collect on her round cheeks and tried to calm her. "They're deep in the undergrowth by now and hightailing it out of here. Were you alone?" he asked. "The only passenger?"

"Alone . . . ?" she was quieting. "Yes. I'm always alone." She drew her chin against her neck and narrowed her eyes. "That Omar! He said . . ." she caught herself and explained. "My husband is Mr. Omar Clay. He brought me out into this wild country and won't go back, even to visit, so every year I make this terrible trip to Kansas City alone." The chin trembled again. "It's the only way I can see my folks. He sticks in that livery stable and fools with those horses." More tears coursed down and she moaned, "Oh, those beasts!"

Orion, not sure if she meant the bandits or Omar's livery horses, stepped past her. He mounted Mick and shouted to Mrs. Clay, "You stay put!" She nodded mutely as he reined Mick into the trees.

There was a clear trail for the first quarter-mile. The bandit had crashed his horse through the underbrush without regard for concealment. Well below the road and along the rim of the canyon, Orion stopped and studied the terrain. A matted growth of low bushes, along with the steep slope, indicated difficult trailing. So, without haste, he returned to the roadway and put Mick into a strong lope. Several miles below the bridge, he turned off into a wash and followed it for half an hour. The wash ended against a well that was half-concealed by a growth of tall willows. The winter run-off water still trickled into a shallow pool. He searched the willows and located a pair of bedrolls and cooking gear. Satisfied, he hid Mick behind the largest willow stand and, armed with his Henry rifle, took a position higher on the bank to wait.

The man with the Wells Fargo box was the first to arrive. Waiting, he peeled a sun-dried bandanna off a wounded hand and patted raw salt into the injured flesh. Orion smiled; his one snap shot had connected. Time dragged on until the sun drifted far enough west to drop a shady curtain into the wash. Orion, cramped but patient, waited until the second man rode in.

"So you made it?" The wounded man was surly.

"My horse bolted, Ben," the other answered cooly. He glanced around and spied the bullion box. "What was all the shootin'?"

"Damn near scared me silly," explained Ben. "That fella just rode up outa nowhere. An' he was a U.S. Marshal. We'd better get along outa here. He's already almost shot off my hand an' he ain't goin' to be settin' still."

"Must be the fella they call Tibbs. Yontz's new

lawman. Don't need to fret. Tibbs hisself is right fresh outa Yuma Prison."

"Bet he knows this country like the palm of his hand," objected Ben. "We'd best divide up and head out—each for hisself."

Orion rose, worked the cramp out of his shoulders and moved silently down the loose bank. The click, as he cocked the Henry, brought both men around. "Best stay where you are," he ordered. "Maybe take one or two steps back from that express box."

Both men froze. Ben was a complete stranger to Orion, but the man last in met his gaze with a knowing leer. "You don't remember me, Orion? Ray Karls? You've still got plenty of savvy, eh, Orion? Figurin' we'd come back here? You remembered it was the only safe camp with regular water in twenty miles?"

Orion nodded wearily. "Only partly right, Ray. Also figured you were still stupid enough to do just that." He motioned to Ben. "I heard you were running with a Ben Griffen."

Offended, Ray Karls flinched like a rattler poked with a stick and snapped, " 'Course we'd come to water first! It's a helluva long ride to the border and . . ."

"The border?" Orion acted surprised. "You sure you don't mean Newt Gobal's Palace Hotel in Pineville?"

Both men dropped their eyes, and while they hesitated Orion issued an order. "Anyway, that's where

you're going. Pineville. And I'm taking in that box
. . ."

"You really gone and swallowed that badge?" Ray
Karls demanded and, as Orion nodded, ejected a
string of curses.

"He gunned me once!" exploded Ben Griffen. "He
ain't doin' it again!" And he went for his gun.

Orion pulled the trigger of the leveled rifle, and
even as the barrel jerked skyward he dove to the
right. Off balance, he triggered two more quick shots.
The first slug caught Ben at the waist and he
clutched both hands to his stomach before rolling
over onto his face. The second shot had knocked Ray
Karls against the bank and the third burned its way
through his brain. Orion approached and looked
down. Both men were dead. The express box—a
small, iron-rimmed wooden box choked with bags of
coin—stood solidly against the crumbling bank.

Orion squatted to study the situation. To the
south was a wide border and a foreign land where a
man could get lost as easily as a flea on a plateau;
there were even extra horses waiting. And what could
anyone ever find out? Mrs. Clay would report two
bandits had bushwhacked the stage, that the marshal
had been hunting them down. Who would ever know
whether he had caught his bandits or had been killed
himself? How could Judge Yontz put out a reward
for a man who might have died trying to recover a
payroll shipment?

Then he remembered the futile wail of Mrs.

Omar Clay, "I'm always alone." Orion glared up at the sky. In an hour it would be dark. He pictured that plump, weepy, little woman alone on the wild, empty road with a dead stagedriver. He grunted. No one could be much more alone than that. It might be days before she would reach Crater Pass . . . Too, there had been the sympathetic blacksmith with whom he had spent the warm afternoon during the choosing of Mick. Could he simply ride one of Omar's horses off, leaving his wife stranded?

Orion chuckled. What a lambasting Omar would get when Mrs. Clay got back to Pineville! You couldn't very well let a man in for that sort of thing, could you?

Without haste, but with the whimsical smile of a man making an idiot of himself, Orion dragged the bullion box a few yards back and kicked down enough gravel to bury the container. He unsaddled the robbers' horses, slapped them into a run, and mounting Mick, rode out.

When Orion Tibbs returned to the stagecoach, Mrs. Omar Clay was pacing nervously in the dusty road. Her face was composed and she had straightened her graying hair. The silver-headed hatpin glinted, holding the bonnet squarely above her wide forehead. She had covered the dead driver with a lap robe but her back was stiff with indignation. Before Orion could explain his delay, she asked with some asperity, "I heard shooting. Was it those bandits?"

He nodded and offered awkwardly, "Sorry to have

left you alone but there was a chance I could run them down."

"I quite understand, Marshal; don't apologize. That husband of mine would have done the same thing. He would . . ." Tears welled up as she continued. "He would have left me alone."

"We'd better get on into Pineville," Orion suggested. "I'll rope a stage horse and you ride Mick. We'll send someone back from the railroad camp to bring in the driver and the stage."

"Those men . . . ?" she asked. "Did—did you kill them?" Clutching her hands together, she waited nervously for his answer.

He shook his head. "Never really got in a good shot." He saw her relief and added to his lie, "They're maybe halfway across the dry lands by now."

Her face suddenly stiffened with disapproval. "But there was a payroll!"

"Bandits depend on gabby stagedrivers," Orion commented drily, then added with resentment, "And I couldn't really stay on their trail and leave you here alone, could I?" He waited until she nodded. "Now, then. Let me help you on my horse and we'll get you on into Pineville."

CHAPTER SIX

Two of Newt Gobal's men huddled out of
the wind, in the lee of a rock wall that circled an
abandoned adobe at the head of Main Street. The
shoddy Mexican hovel, wasted by weather, was now a
lump of shadows in the cloudy night.

"Newt could have just let the damned marshal ride
in. We could've took him any time. It's cold as hell
. . ."

"Shh!" the second man cautioned, raising his
head over the wall to stare into darkness. "Someone's
coming. Sounds like two horses."

"Let me see." The speaker edged his way to the
end of the wall and waited. Several minutes passed
before he flagged his partner forward. "It's Tibbs, all
right, an' he's got a woman with him. Nobody said
anything about any woman."

"We can't help that. We got orders. When you step
out I'll circle around behind. If he goes for his gun,
we'll fire together. I know it's plenty risky, but the
woman'll just have to take her chances."

Nodding, the second man clambered over the wall,
threw a cartridge into the rifle breech and shouted,
"Marshal, halt your horse! Keep your hands on your
saddlehorn. My partner's going to come up and take

your guns. You'd better do just what we say if you don't want that woman hurt!"

Orion Tibbs had begun to edge his horse away from Mrs. Clay when he felt the muzzle press firmly into his backbone. He turned his head slowly. The man had one hand on Mick's flank and the other on the rifle trigger. Mrs. Clay's face was chalky with alarm. He felt his Colt jerked from the holster. "What's this all about?" he asked easily.

"You'll see, Mr. Marshal. We're from a vigilante committee. There's others waiting down at The Palace."

Orion sighed. It had been a rough trip. The long ride from the robbery site with a voluble Mrs. Clay, then the angry explosions from Roger Allan when he learned that the railroad payroll had been stolen. The engineer's ill-concealed suspicions had been supported by railroad workers, whose curses grew violent when they learned their pay had again been delayed. Orion had brushed them aside, picked up a riding horse for Mrs. Clay and now, when he'd thought he was finishing a long, hard day, this had to happen. Two men with leveled rifles, prepared to shoot him down if he resisted. And, ahead, some sort of "kangaroo court" waited.

"So the vigilantes are waiting?" Heat gathered in his voice. "What's the charge?"

"Bushwhackin' Roddy Ryan . . ."

It made him laugh. Mick, startled, raised his head and Orion twisted away from the sudden pressure of the rifle

"Don't do that again!" The rifleman was angry and added viciously, "You do an' you'll go in as a corpse, belly down!"

"Then let's go on in," answered Orion, "while we're all in the saddle."

"Shooting an unarmed man ain't healthy in this country," snapped the second captor. "Nobody remembers seein' Roddy with a gun." The voice was almost jovially bitter. "An' Doc Saber says Roddy was killed by a slug in the back!"

Main Street was suspiciously quiet all the way to The Palace. There, like popcorn in a covered container, the sudden hush covering the town was wiped away. A loud piano boomed out the "Oceana Roll" and men shouted as they circled tables to get to the bar. Three bartenders were busy filling glasses and wiping the sloshed liquor off the bar.

The news of Orion's capture had raced ahead, and excitement flared when it was learned the marshal was being brought in with a woman. Newt Gobal, a perplexed frown on his ruddy face, waited on the porch as the group rode in. When he caught sight of Mrs. Clay, he pushed his way into the crowd. "Mrs. Clay!" he exclaimed. "What under the sun are you doing with 'Killer' Tibbs?" He reached up to help her off the horse but she angrily reined away and joggled off in the direction of the livery stable. Newt guffawed up at Orion. "When the chips are down, the ladies don't wait around. Eh, Marshal?"

Before he could reply, Orion was jerked from the saddle and hoisted up the short stairs. He looked back. The street, except for a crowd surging around the front of the hotel, was empty. Mrs. Clay's horse was outlined by the light in Omar Clay's shop where the stack threw sparks into the night. His lips lifted wryly. The years in prison had dulled his wits. When he'd ridden the "hoot owl" trail, he would have smelled the danger hidden near the old adobe. Yet it had happened, and now, as excited men yanked him into the crowded barroom, he controlled his anger and waited alertly for a chance to break free.

Newt Gobal had ordered the tables pushed back against the walls and now, with a cold fury barely concealed, he was ready to open the "kangaroo court." "Let me have your attention!" Newt shouted, but the crowd paid little heed. Excited voices and the clink of bottles and glasses overrode Newt's words. Finally, with a bung starter, he banged the bar and shouted, "Vigilante court's in session. Damn-it-all-to-hell! Quit your gabbing! Find seats or places against the wall. We got to have space to give this killer a fair trial!"

When he had partial attention, he lowered his voice and began the indictment. "We're here to judge a criminal. This U.S. Marshal, Orion Tibbs, brought into Pineville by our psalm-singing circuit judge, has committed deliberate murder and . . ."

"We know all about that. Cut the speeches!" A tipsy man yelled.

Newt ignored the remark and continued. "And we all know that Tibbs shot Roddy Ryan in the back." His words brought a cheer and he held up both hands for quiet. "We're here to judge the killer and apply proper judgment. Nobody really seen the shooting. Roddy's Colt was never found. And . . ."

"*Un momento,* Newt Gobal. We'd better do this thing right," warned a tall man. Orion swung around and saw the speaker was young, barely out of his teens. His face was raddled with pockmarks but he carried his new rifle like it was an old friend.

"We're doing just that, Calaway," Newt growled, and tried to pin the young man's eyes with a threatening stare. "All that's needed is a look at the facts. Anyone can see he's a killer so—we take him out and hang him."

Calaway slowly shook his head in disagreement. "First there's got to be a jury. If a man's faced with lynching, he's entitled to two things. A fair trial or"— Calaway grinned into Newt Gobal's glare—"a gun so's he can try to shoot his way out. Now to give him a fair trial means we got to appoint us a jury. Guilty or not, there's got to be a jury. Later on, folks is gonna ask—did he have a fair trial? Understand?" Calaway turned his boyish smile onto Orion Tibbs while the babble broke out again.

Orion began to understand Calaway's move. The rifleman's name meant nothing, but the bold posture, the calm yet aggressive statements, gave him some hope his force might control. Calaway, obviously dangerous in any situation, had raised a protective screen in front of the accused. A jury might hesitate to order a hanging. Mob action, a hurried lynching by infuriated men, was sometimes condoned by honest citizens. On the other hand, the men on a selected jury could be singled out after a hanging. They would have to defend their decision and live with it. Arizona's territorial law might be slow, but it could move ponderously and eventually challenge the decision of such an illegal lynching. Such jury members could become the accused and be tried for the death they had sanctioned.

Newt sensed Calaway's strategy and fought it. "Look," he growled, "we all know Tibbs shot Roddy in the back. And he's been convicted for such killings before. Yontz brought him here to support his own type of law and, right off, while the judge was present, Tibbs did his killing. Didn't he? Didn't he put a slug in Roddy's back?"

Calaway faced around very slowly. His muscular hand was taut on the rifle breech and every man in the room could see how the forefinger rode the trigger. The room stilled. Finally Newt conceded with a shout, "Then let's pick us a jury and hang Tibbs legal! We'll draw lots. Let the bartender mark twelve playing cards and chuck the deck in a hat. The twelve men drawing the marked cards are the jurymen. That satisfy you, Calaway?" Calaway shrugged a grim assent, threw a tight smile at Tibbs, and moved back against the wall.

This new development calmed the crowd. Some men visibly hesitated, hoping cards would be drawn before their turn came around. Others, more hardened or on nods from Newt Gobal, moved quickly into a line. Someone shoved a chair forward, and

Tibbs was pushed down while his ankles were bound to the chair legs.

As the jurymen were being picked, twelve chairs were lined up alongside the piano, a table was placed near the center of the room and finally the "kangaroo court" was in full session.

"As previously stated," Newt Gobal, throwing Calaway a look of triumph, started, "we are gathered together to bring out testimony that one Roddy Ryan, constable of Pineville, was shot in the back by Orion Tibbs. We'll call Dr. Saber as our first witness. Doctor, will you step forward?"

Dr. Saber was a waif of a man. His scarred derby hat failed to conceal the lank but thinning hair which crept down to his coat collar. Under different conditions, the doctor might have made a more favorable appearance, but here in this ornate barroom of the Palace Hotel, his full lips still wet from whiskey, he was a befuddled old man. Like many loners, he'd been used up by the rigors of the Western territory. Now, for a drink and a slap on the back—or a threat from Newt Gobal—he was prepared to call Orion Tibbs a killer. Even more, he was willing to lie a U.S. Marshal into a lynching.

"Dr. Saber, are you ready to tell us all you discovered when you tried to save Roddy Ryan's life?" Newt began his questioning.

"To the best of my ability." Dr. Saber swayed and peered owlishly at Newt before he directed his wavering attention to the prisoner.

"Did you examine and treat Roddy Ryan, Doctor?"

"To the best of my ability," Saber repeated loftily. His answer brought a chuckle from the tense crowd.

Orion Tibbs felt a nudge from behind and turned. Calaway grinned down and quipped softly, "What a place we got to live in. A drunk for a doctor—I wouldn't let him treat my horse—and a U.S. Marshal who shoots constables in the back."

"And Newt Gobal running the show," added Tibbs grimly. He turned back to watch and listen to Dr. Saber.

"Then tell us, Doctor, all you know." Newt led the man on, taking time to shoot a gloating glance at Tibbs.

"Roddy Ryan was brought to my office with a gunshot wound." He held a cracked fingernail against his chest. "The slug entered the back between the shoulder blades, and erupted through the breastbone. When I served as surgeon in the cavalry, such wounds were considered lethal and the patient was given a swallow of laudanam and permitted to die in peace. However, I made every effort to cleanse and close Ryan's wound. In spite of my best efforts, he died."

"Satisfied?" Newt Gobal dismissed Dr. Saber, then added, "We have one more witness." He raised up and located his man. "We'll call forward a hotel employee, Art Peaker, who helped carry Roddy to the doctor's office. Art, step forward to the table."

Peaker, still dressed in grease-stained buckskins, had also seen better days. His buffalo-skinning work was over, and for the past year he'd spent his waking hours cleaning slops and spittoons in various areas around the hotel. Peaker, keeping bleary eyes focused on Newt's face, desperately prayed he would remember the right answers.

"Art," Newt began carefully, "when you carried Roddy to Doc Sabers . . ."

"Aye," Art interrupted.

"Did you find Roddy's gun?"

"Like you told me, he don't have a gun," Art Peaker answered quickly. Someone in the room snickered and Art, without removing his eyes from Newt's face, added his own lugubrious grimace.

"No gun. Are you sure, Art?"

Indecision flagged across the swamper's face and his bleary eyes filled with moisture. "No gun, Mr. Gobal, I swear it. For *sure* he don't have no gun." Shaking, the witness shuffled toward the bar. Newt gave the bartender a quick nod, and a brimming glass was waiting when the grubby witness reached out a clawed hand.

Newt rose and advanced, laying a forearm over the top of the piano as he gazed over the room. "That's our case, gentlemen of the jury. We've brought in proof that Roddy Ryan was shot in the back. Doc Saber testified to that. Art Peaker proved Roddy was unarmed." He turned slowly and, with unctuous sympathy, asked the marshal, "Would you like to add anything to that?"

Orion Tibbs leaned back in the chair and studied Newt Gobal's tense features. Death was mirrored in the narrow eyes. Hate, like an adder's flicking tongue, wet the thick lips. Controlled madness, an almost frenzied recklessness, filled the man. It was as though he was testing his power in leading a group of men to accept contrived evidence to take a man's life, solely because Newt Gobal wanted it done. Others sensed this and the room stilled as men leaned forward to hear the marshal's reply.

A movement at the doorway caught Orion's attention. Omar Clay, solid as a rock, holding two sawed-off shotguns in his big blacksmith's hands, the barrels still shiny from the file, waved the gun muzzles, which seemed to be aimed at everyone who turned to look. "*I'm* not satisfied, Newt," Omar stated flatly, "and I won't be satisfied until you either untie the marshal—or I trigger all four barrels of these twin cannons!"

CHAPTER SEVEN

Judge Leander Yontz heard the astounding news from Pineville, at Clay Mountain. It was only the second day of his tour, so he had to accept the delay philosophically until he finished the circuit. On the afternoon of the fifth day, he drove his lathered team into Pineville and halted them in front of the marshal's office. Omar Clay, shotgun at hip level, strolled out of the shade from the south side of the building.

"Marshal Tibbs around, Omar?"

"Right inside, Judge," Omar replied and walked quickly back out of sight.

Yontz, tight-lipped, stepped out of the buggy and knocked on the rough door. "Tibbs? This is Yontz. You want to open up?"

The marshal opened the door and stood aside for the judge to enter. "Come right in, Judge." Tibbs was holding the most vicious weapon the judge had ever seen—a riot gun with barrels so short he could almost see the loads. Such a weapon could blow a man apart at five feet and injure any man in front— or to the side—of the possessor. Yontz stared past into the narrow aisle between the cells. The two cells were crammed to the bars with prisoners. Sullen voices cursed vain threats. The place was heavy with foul air. "As bad," he muttered, "as the 'Black Hole of Calcutta.' "

"How many you got locked up in here?" Yontz asked.

"Only thirty-five of the worst, Judge. The rest had to be handcuffed and leg-ironed to the corral posts. I have Omar Clay watching out back. Altogether, we're holding fifty-five prisoners."

"Interesting, Marshal. What do you propose doing with them?"

"I figured that was your end of the deal, Judge. You set up court and we'll give them a trial . . ."

"Try us, hell!" Newt Gobal's angry voice rang out from the back. "You let us out. We ain't hogs to be held in no hogpen!"

Judge Yontz stepped into the corridor. Newt Gobal elbowed his way to the cell door and shouted, "We been in here three days. That crazy Tibbs just keeps that rock gun pointed down here and keeps sayin', 'Wait'll Yontz gets back.' "

Orion interrupted with a chuckle. "The boys down at Territorial could do three days standing on their hands."

Yontz, tight-lipped, motioned the marshal to follow and left the jail. He led the way over to the hotel. From the window of the judge's room, Tibbs waved a reassuring hand to Omar Clay. Then he turned back and waited for the judge to break his silence.

"That's a pretty big bite, Orion. You'd better give me the details." Yontz settled back in a cane-bottomed chair.

In terse detail, Tibbs told of his capture, the farce of the "kangaroo court," and the fortuitous rescue by Omar Clay. Arrogantly, he finished, "And we just marched them over and threw them all in jail."

"Three days ago?" asked Yontz. Orion nodded, a bit uncertain at the judge's sulky mien.

"And what did you charge them with?" Yontz asked sourly.

"Attempted murder and theft." Defensively, Tibbs added, "Theft of my rifle and Colt."

"Only two of them stole your weapons . . ." Suddenly, Yontz began to smile, then broke into a hearty laugh. He moved out of the chair and searched his littered highboy for a bottle. Pouring two drinks, he extended a brimming glass, then resumed his seat. "The rest—including Gobal—can beat any charge of attempted murder. The facts prove that Omar arrived before the 'kangaroo court' could harm you. Any judge would give them a slap on the wrist and turn them loose. We'll just change the charge to a misdemeanor, obstructing an officer, and give 'em three days in jail."

"You mean, count the three days they've already served?" Orion asked with some heat.

"That's it, Marshal. Sound like a fair deal to you?" He held up a hand to halt Orion's protest and added, "The two who brought you in we give three days and orders to leave Pineville."

Orion Tibbs stiffened and began pacing the small room. Yontz didn't wait for an answer. "Looks like you had Pineville under 'Marshal' law!" He finished his whiskey in a gulp and rose to leave, but Orion halted him in mid-stride with a curse.

"I want you to know, Judge," he said coldly, "if you won't try them, I'll take them into Tucson! Now wait a damned minute, Judge! When you bailed me out of Yuma, you wanted a gunslinger. I was supposed to make Gobal's crew toe the line. Well, we've got them off balance so let's keep them rolling. Something like this happens in Mexico and they chain them all together and march them off to the capitol. Those who arrive, are too damned battered to do more than beg. That's what these . . ."

"Don't tell me my business!" shouted the judge. The worry churning his stomach had turned to definite anger at the marshal's proposal. "Don't forget you're under my orders. Act within reason or you'll damned well go back to prison. I said we'll turn 'em loose and that's just what you're going to do!"

"Then I'm riding out!" Orion shot back.

"Ride out!" Yontz slapped the glass down and whirled. "I'll have a poster on you and the bounty hunters'll pick you up before you reach the border!"

"I know the Tooloons, Judge. There're places in there where your bounty hunters had better stay out!"

"Now, Orion"—Yontz's face smoothed out—"there's too much involved for you to go off half-cocked. The fact is—you *can't* ride out." He watched uncertainty cross the marshal's face. "Omar Clay saved your life when the vigilante committee was

ready to string you up; you'll have to stay if only to
protect Omar. If nothing else he's earned his right to
be protected by the law. On top of that—and I don't
really know if it means a damned thing to you—I put
my reputation on the line when I made you a U.S.
Marshal. There's something big going on and it's got
to be headed off. My court's no good without your
backing. All I'm asking, Orion Tibbs, is that you let
me call the shots." He turned away to pour another
drink.

Orion cooled off slowly. Freeing Newt Gobal and
the rest of his crew seemed stupid, but was it? Lately,
Orion had been wondering if he really understood
right from wrong. He had gunned down the stage
bandits, yet instead of scooting for Mexico with the
loot, he'd trotted back with Mrs. Clay in tow. Why?
Killing the bandits had been within the authority of
a marshal, but he'd acted like a criminal by hiding
the railroad payroll. And of course he did owe something to the sleepy-eyed blacksmith who had pulled
him out of the squeeze at the "kangaroo court." Why
did it need Yontz to remind him of his obligation to
Omar? Maybe he had better stick around for a while
and he just might learn from Yontz and Omar Clay.
As Yontz watched closely, Orion shrugged, then in a
gruff tone capitulated. "We'd better go on down and
let those poor criminals out of their cells."

The following week passed without Yontz's prophesied trouble. The townsmen who faced the judge
bore the verbal lashes of a very exasperated court.
Newt Gobal tried to bluster, but the judge quickly

offered him the opportunity to plead guilty or to take Tibbs' suggested march into Tucson, and Newt quickly agreed to a guilty plea. The story of Marshal Tibbs and his fifty-five-man jail, spread through the Territory, and people wondered aloud if maybe they shouldn't allow more Territorial prisoners to take over law officer positions.

Gunfighters, looking for a reputation or a future contest, lodged Orion Tibbs' name deep in their memory. Wells Fargo sent several manhunters into the Tooloons in search of the stage bandits. They searched, but reported back that the pair must have successfully made the crossing into Mexico.

Peggy Smith entertained at The Palace. She danced with the patrons and filled in with practiced flirting expected of a saloon girl. As the week ended and Pineville settled down, Orion Tibbs, returning from an evening visit with Omar and Mrs. Clay, found Peggy seated on the cool back balcony. The squeak of her rocking chair against the sun-dried boards told him someone was in the dark corner. He stepped over and peered down. Peggy had drawn her arms under her green shawl and was sobbing softly. She was dressed in an ankle-length skirt of maroon with a white shirtwaist. Her hair, pulled into a tight coil, gave her a young and sedate look. Orion liked this attire much better than her customary dancing costume.

"I heard you crying," he began uneasily. "Sometimes women cry louder at good news than bad. Which is it with you, Peggy?"

"It doesn't matter." She straightened and as though aware of his drawing back, added quickly, "Women sometimes cry for nothing. Or for something that happened a long time ago. Like— well, like when a man needs to get drunk. Sometimes women can cry it out."

"I see . . ."

She laughed at his impassiveness, dabbed her eyes with a handkerchief, and sat up straight in the chair. Orion leaned against the balcony, then broke the silence. "Were you born out West?"

"Good Lord, no!" She looked out at the mountains. The Tooloons were black and threatening under a dim moon. Sand and twigs, worried loose by the ever-present wind, rattled against the boughs of the sagebrush. A gentle but pungent smell of tarweed and greasewood intermingled. "Where I was born," she went on, "you could hear the sea. Tall trees, tall enough to make into spars, threw the sound of the wind back into the sea. So different from this desert land, so shut in by distance. It—makes me lonely and . . ." She laughed again. "So, I cry."

"Enjoy yourself." He stepped back from the railing to move off.

"Stay and talk," she begged, then quickly added, "How about you, Marshal? Where do you come from?"

It took him a second to remember. "We left Richmond, Virginia, when I was fourteen years old. Crossing the Panama Isthmus, we were on the way to Oregon. . . . My father was killed by Cholo Indians. I lit out. When I learned to use a gun, I spent the next five years working around in Mexico. I took bounty, mostly Apache scalps, for awhile. Then . . ." He smiled thinly at her grimace of distaste. He hadn't talked to a real woman for so long he suddenly felt as though he was rattling on. "Then I went out on my own and ended up in Territorial Prison for killing a banker."

"It doesn't pay bounty to kill bankers," she said lightly.

"Not unless you get away with the loot," he quipped. Naturally, he thought, she had jumped to the conclusion he had been robbing a bank and felt it necessary to explain. "I was *protecting* the banker. I was hired to ride along while he drove out to a ranch with some money and we were jumped. The banker was killed and they shot me all to pieces. Nobody believed I wasn't part of it. They wanted a fall guy and I was it. I was charged with murder and sent to prison."

"I guess it could happen that way . . ." Her voice had lost its warmth and he could feel her withdrawal. What had been a pleasant chat was now chilled by her suspicions.

"Hard story to believe?" he asked, quietly.

In the dark she shook her head and her answer was gentle. "That must have been awful. To be accused and punished without . . ."

"Without ever getting the money?" he interrupted,

then added with some logic, "Not so bad, really. There were plenty of other times I'd earned a prison sentence or even a hanging."

She was silent and he knew she was weighing. How many such stories had she listened to? How many men had used her as a sounding board and drifted on? "Excuse me now, Peggy. Unless," he offered hopefully, "you would like to join me in a drink?"

She shook her head slowly. "Maybe later, Marshal. Judge Yontz told me to wait right here until he comes."

"Then you do just that!" Without looking back, Orion Tibbs strode away.

CHAPTER EIGHT

The same night, several hours after he left Peggy Smith waiting for the judge, Orion had a run-in with four of Piper Garfield's cowboys. Garfield was moving his herd to winter grass in the Tooloon foothills and the men had been sent ahead for supplies. Their spree had started slowly, but as it gathered momentum on whiskey and tequila, the marshal was called in to clear the boisterous waddies out of Raphael's back street Cantina.

While Orion was disarming the cowboys, Carey, the straw boss, turned cantankerous and caught a slug in his shoulder. Carey mouthed off, threatening to ride into Pineville with fifty Garfield men and shoot off the Marshal's ears.

A night in jail could have settled the matter and Orion Tibbs might never have crossed swords with Piper Garfield but Garfield, who ruled thousands of acres like a despot and raised the largest herd in the territory, carrying his pride on his sleeve, now decided to back up Carey's threat. Once the herd was bedded down on the old buffalo grounds, Garfield led his pugnacious crew into town.

Orion was having his morning coffee alone in the office. Carey, patched up by Dr. Saber, was the sole occupant of the first cell. Piper Garfield, followed by a half-dozen men, swaggered in and glared down at the marshal. "You want to turn Carey loose now," he demanded, "or after I pull your jail apart?"

"As soon as he pays for the damages to Raphael's Cantina, he can leave," Orion said easily.

"You're the boss, Marshal," Garfield replied and turned paymaster. "Trot over to Raphael's and get a bill for damages." He turned back to Tibbs with deceptive frankness. "Now, you unlock the cell and let my man out."

Orion nodded. As he stepped around the end of the desk to reach for the keys, Garfield raised the handle of a lead-filled quirt and struck out with all the force of his heavy arms. Orion took the blow on a raised shoulder and stumbled to the wall. Garfield drew up on his boot toes to smash again. Orion raised both arms over his head to the rafter, stepped aside, and shoved the muzzle of a shotgun forward; he pulled the trigger and one barrel belched iron. Garfield, quirt halted in mid-air, backed off and ducked. The pungent smoke of the explosion filled the room and men scrambled to escape. Garfield's hat whirled into a corner, a single pellet raked his temple and a trickle of blood traced a stubbly cheek. Eyes narrowed in shock, too stunned to move further, Garfield lowered his quirt and groggily tried to avoid the weapon's second barrel. It was pointed directly into the cattleman's face, and he viewed the lethal opening with horror.

Orion Tibbs' granite-hard face softened as he clamped a thumb over the hammer and slowly eased it off. Slowly, he reached over to the desk, picked up another shotgun shell and reloaded. Garfield's frozen face worked as he waited for Orion to speak.

"Now I've got to locate another hideout," Orion said softly. "Can't work a surprise like this but once." He grinned, then added. "You can go, Cattle King."

Garfield was slowly pulling himself together. Orion could read his opponent's mind. Once Garfield walked out the door without Carey his reputation was tarnished, perhaps ruined. This gruff lord of the Arizona grasslands had been literally lifted by his suspenders and shaken like some whining kid. It intrigued Orion. What would Garfield do? The men waiting outside, no longer panicked, would be looking for a fight, expecting to storm the jail and kill themselves a U.S. Marshal. They were waiting for Garfield's orders.

"I said"—Orion pushed the pin into Piper Garfield's pride a bit deeper—"you can go." He stepped around the still-stunned man and recovered his hat, half-destroyed by the gunshot, the head-band flopping. "Cattle King," he said flatly, clapping the hat onto Garfield's head, "you're not welcome in my jail."

Recovering, Garfield wiped the blood on the back of a furious hand, straightened the hat, then exploded. "I'm going! But, the minute you step outside, you're a dead man!" The threat brought back a bit of bravado and he added, "There'll be fifty guns to drill you and I'll pay bounty for every slug that hits." Without waiting for an answer, he sucked in a deep breath and strode out.

Orion followed to the door, holding the shotgun at hip level. He nudged Garfield aside and addressed the cattle crew. "Clear out of here!" He raised his voice and waved the weapon. "The show's over!" He watched as Garfield pushed a path through the glowering men and led them into the Palace Bar.

The sound of the anvil echoed through the scraggly wooden wall of Omar Clay's barn. A puff of black smoke rose above the distant Crater Pass. Pineville was enjoying an ominous hour of quiet. Judge Yontz and Orion Tibbs squatted in the sun and idly watched the frisky livery horses. Both men were outwardly calm but their divergent opinions, openly argued, had them both edgy.

Yontz was heatedly repeating himself. "You've got to let that Carey out of jail. The damage has been paid and there's just no charge to hold him on. Holding him as a hostage is a pure violation of his rights. Only Indians hold hostages . . ."

Orion interrupted, keeping his temper even. "If I let him out Garfield will turn loose his guns. I'm responsible for the peace and safety of this town."

"Then it's Garfield who should be arrested," argued Yontz. He caught the narrowing look in the marshal's eyes and hastily continued. "But—don't think of anything like that!"

Orion was losing his temper. "We've been over this. It's hold Carey until Garfield has to move his herd, or else fight his whole damned crew. Soon as I let Carey out they'll come shooting."

"You never should have arrested him!" Yontz snapped, then recanted. "Now, now, Orion, I'll take some of that back. But my whole plan seems to be coming apart. It went wrong when I told you to run Roddy Ryan out. I could have issued an official order for him to vacate and . . ."

"He'd have stayed put!" The fumbling logic of the judge was becoming irritating and Orion turned sarcastic. "Your Honor knows that Roddy was working for Newt Gobal and they'd both have told you to go to hell!"

"Maybe so . . ." Yontz answered moodily. "Still, since Roddy died, will you please look at what's happened? Newt Gobal and his 'kangaroo court' spent three days in jail. The railroad payroll was stolen. You were damned near lynched. Piper Garfield and his cattle crew declared war on Pineville—and on you!" He stared at the corral of horses. "Who's guarding the jail?" he suddenly asked.

"Calaway. He gave me some help the night they had me ready to pluck. Calaway's got orders to gut-shoot Carey if anyone tries to break him out."

"Will he do that?" Yontz stared hard at the marshal, beginning to ask himself what kind of man he had brought out of Yuma. Was Tibbs walking a tightrope for some reason of his own? And had he enlisted Calaway? The marshal's explanation brought fear into the judge's face.

"Calaway," Orion replied, "was in Territoral Prison too, Judge. He won't stand for nonsense. He'll kill Carey if Garfield even starts across the street."

"My God!" groaned Judge Yontz. "Now Pineville has two ex-convicts as lawmen." He stiffened and raised his voice in judicial authority. "There's one way out. You take Calaway and go out hunting those stage robbers. Stay out at least three weeks. Then you contact me before you return!"

Orion shrugged. It was one answer, he supposed. The Garfield herds would be on winter graze and things would have a chance to cool down. Garfield couldn't afford to tie up his army of waddies for three weeks. Three days in jail had cooled Newt Gobal off. The hotel owner had been pretty quiet and many of his followers had drifted off. Orion put his doubt into words. "It sure would've been tough, Judge, if Newt and Garfield had teamed up." One doubt he held back. Garfield just might take his revenge out on the judge. With Carey released, and the marshal out of town, Garfield would have a perfect chance to smash Pineville and could even vent his spleen on Yontz. There was one way, Orion mused, to keep Garfield busy. Only a couple of men could spook a mighty big herd.

"Piper wouldn't go along with Gobal," Yontz barked. "Gobal's men have been rustling Arizona cattle for the last five years." He continued, allowing anger to loosen his tongue. "Can't you see what's really going on? Gobal runs one whole strata in this country; he makes the plans and brings in the men. He's got his web stretched clear to the Mexican border and that's why he fights the railroad. The tracks will settle this country, will limit Gobal's operations and finally choke him off. Every gunslinger out here knows that." He paused and threw the marshal a sneering glance. "Why, Newt Gobal could raise an army in a week that could wipe Arizona clean!"

Orion accepted the judge's pronouncement with his tongue in his cheek. "Looks like Garfield could do the same."

"Of course he could. However, Piper is an honest man; hard and vengeful but honest. He's got backing from every rancher and even from the governor. Piper Garfield wants the railroad but he won't accept Pineville as a terminal. Gobal's land, understand? Like another hole-in-the-wall country."

"So Roger Allan's railroad is caught in the middle? Newt doesn't want the railroad but he's going to get it right in his lap!"

"There's some bets against that," groaned the judge.

"You think Gobal got the payroll?" Orion quizzed. "Or maybe Piper Garfield? To slow things down?"

"What's the use of talking about it?" Yontz rose and stretched his legs. "You take Calaway and both of you get out of Pineville for awhile. Who knows, you might even locate those stage bandits."

"We'll go along," agreed Orion. "But a couple of stagecoach bandits won't help Roger Allan very much. He needs the payroll. Calaway and me will ride herd on the next shipment of railroad coin, Judge."

Yontz's face, suddenly erased of strain, showed small laugh wrinkles building around the wise old eyes. "If you can sell that idea to Wells Fargo," he smiled, "it's fine with me."

An early storm, sagging with rain and black with thunder, had ballooned out of the east. Thunder followed the lightning and released slashing torrents. Dawn found the sky still black, but the sun had found a hole to poke a golden finger through the cloud rifts. The wind in the high mountains had scattered new deadfalls and still whispered through quivering branches.

Orion Tibbs guided Mick and the pack horse through the deepening water in a canyon high in the Tooloons. Calaway, weakened by loss of blood from a stomach wound clung to his saddlehorn. The dead weight disturbed Mick but the horse pressed his muzzle against Orion's arm and, belly deep, lunged against the water-covered boulders.

They left the canyon and reached a small meadow beneath the rimrock. It was an acre of lush grass, spaced by willows and buffalo grass. Flattened against rocky rimrock shoulders and half-concealed by undergrowth, a weathered log cabin came into view. A stovepipe, steadied by barbed wire, angled away from the rocky overhang. The builders had desired concealment and had blended the cabin into the setting.

"It's the place, Cal," Orion said and took the wounded man's weight onto his shoulder. "We'll get you inside, get a fire going and see what can be done about that slug."

"A good place to butcher slow elk," grunted Calaway. "You do know your way around, Marshal," he added, with respect.

"A Zuni fish hunter showed me the Tooloons. Zuni like to live in houses. We built this cabin."

Pain silenced Calaway until they entered the cabin and he relaxed on the shabby bunk. With gritted teeth and some exasperation with his own helplessness, Calaway waited for the pain to subside, then spoke again. "I've helped spook herds before but this was a dinger. Garfield's herd must be spread all over these mountains."

"Now Garfield won't be sitting around making trouble for the judge," Orion stated, breaking a few twigs and lighting the fireplace.

In an hour, the cabin was warm. The pocket-sized fireplace and a pine torch, jabbed in the mouth of a demijohn, provided enough light for Orion to examine Calaway's wound. The slug had blunted against the hip bone, shattered it and raked upward. Blood still seeped from the flap of bruised and torn skin. Orion drew back, hiding concern. "You're still carrying the slug. It must've shattered. Maybe I should bring out Doc Saber?"

"From what I've seen of that old butcher, Marshal, you can't do worse. Have at it."

"Once we get the slug, Cal, we'll have to cauterize the wound with powder. Can you stand up to it?"

"No choice," Calaway answered. Orion nodded and began to hone his pocketknife.

CHAPTER NINE

The next two weeks brought fall weather into the mountains. Scrub oaks and yellowing elms shed their leaves while the wild vines turned gold and purple. The nights were colder and mornings brought fog dripping steadily from the trees. The sun gave just enough warmth to raise vapor from shake roofs and turned the grass green. In spite of the perfect weather, Calaway's wound did not respond to treatment.

Calaway's side had swollen and the skin turned blue. He developed a fever and Orion spent hours compressing the wound in order to reduce the high fever, which was causing partial stupor and some raving. Orion, watching Calaway's struggle for life, knew a medical man was needed but was afraid to leave the patient.

The long days gave him time to think, to look back. It had been his own idea to stampede the Garfield herd, a sort of defiant act to show both Garfield and Judge Yontz; to show Garfield his threats meant little and for Yontz to discover that a marshal, even if he was an ex-convict, could find ways to fight back. Calaway had joined in exuberantly, happy simply to raise hell and cause a little excitement. Now Calaway was down with a bad wound and his chances were poor.

The judge shouldn't have ordered them out of Pineville. A head-on battle with Garfield would have brought the matter to an end. Orion shook his head with self-disgust. Why all the concern about Leander Yontz? The judge hadn't done any favors by snatching a convict out of Yuma. The judge was only thinking about the damned territory; the opening of the land by railroad and controlling people like Newt Gobal. He had simply gone out and obtained the best instrument to do a job—a killing tool, one to be controlled by a fear of returning to prison. Don't ask questions, killer! Just do what you're told or, by God, I'll snatch your parole away!

Orion knew now he should have taken the Wells Fargo box and raced for the border. With plenty of money and the contacts he had, he could have become a *Don* with a *ranchero* as large as a man could travel in a day. And why hadn't he? Simply because Mrs. Clay had been left alone beside the wrecked stage with a dead driver. The thought of the terrified and forlorn woman on a wild mountain road had caused him to bury the express box and ride back into Pineville. Then his intention had been to deliver Mrs. Clay and return to the cache. However, Newt Gobal's vigilante committee and Garfield's anger had delayed his escape into Mexico. Now he was stuck up on the rimrock with a dying deputy. A thought struck him. He didn't owe Calaway anything. It had been Omar Clay who rescued him from the "kangaroo court." Calaway had stayed aloof, twiddling his rifle, letting the farce go on. Calaway himself, if their positions were reversed, would have ridden out, picked up the payroll and skedaddled. Orion heard the wounded man muttering and stepped to the side of the bunk.

Calaway's eyes were murky. He hooked a whitened hand onto the overhead lath and tried to pull himself into a sitting position. Orion nodded with relief. "It's about time you came back to life."

Calaway focused. "You still hanging around, Marshal?" he asked. "I'd have been across the border."

"I thought about it," admitted Orion, realizing Calaway had guessed the truth about the stage holdup.

"Caught in between?"

"I guess so." Grimacing, Orion dropped his eyes to the badge. "What made you think I got the payroll?"

"You had to have it, Marshal, because Newt's boys never came back." His eyes closed in pain.

"Did Newt expect a cut?"

Calaway ignored the question. "Newt thinks you gunned them down and hid the payroll—'cause you was dam'fool enough to bring in Clay's old woman. That about right?"

"Pretty close," admitted Orion.

"I knew both those boys," Calaway rambled on. "They'd never run off and miss the big raid . . ." Apologetically, he added, "You must have figured by now why I joined with you."

Orion straightened with surprise. Calaway wasn't a windjammer. Any man who spent years on the night-owl trail stayed alive because he could keep his mouth shut, and Calaway *had* been one of Newt's gang until Garfield had swaggered into the picture. Only then had he maneuvered around to join with the law by acting as jailer for Carey. Newt Gobal, hating the cattleman, naturally wouldn't object. A schemer like Newt would be glad to place a man in position to spy on the marshal.

Orion ignored Calaway's guess about the cache. *"The big raid?"* he asked. "That payroll was pretty big money. What could Newt offer that would pay any better?"

Calaway tried to answer. His lips moved convulsively and his body strained to rise. Even as Orion pressed the pain-wracked body down, the man under his hand died.

Orion moved away from the bunk. The fire crackled and the faint song of the wind whistled through a broken window. Calaway's death would leave him free to gather in the payroll and run for freedom, yet Calaway's talk about the "big raid" was confusing. Orion cursed to himself. Nothing had been simple since he had been bailed out of Yuma. Yontz's belief that a paroled gunslinger could straighten out the problems the railroad had opened up was a pretty ambitious belief. And now, adding to his confusion, was this talk of a "big raid" and Cala-way's death. He had liked the man; evidently Cala-way had returned the feeling. With his last breath, believing Orion Tibbs was trying to become an honest lawman, Calaway had passed on information about some big crime Newt Gobal was plotting. What should he do now? Orion rose in self-anger and stomped outside to locate Mick.

The clatter of a running horse reached Orion as he led Mick, with Calaway's body, into a stand of tamarack and waited. The rider approached, then drew even. Orion, rifle raised, stepped out into the roadway. "Hold it right there, mister!" he called out. "Just step down and explain your big hurry."

Nervously, the rider stared and finally recognized the marshal. "All hell's busted loose! That crazy Garfield's got the town surrounded and he's threatening to burn it out. Newt sent some of us out for help."

"What's Garfield riled about now?" Orion asked innocently.

"His herd was spooked and stampeded all over northern Arizona! Garfield wants Newt's hide but Newt claims he didn't move no hand in it. And he ain't backin' off from no showdown with Garfield. Understand, Marshal? So if you'll take your rifle off me, I'll get on!"

Orion waved him past. This country was as explosive as a match in a powder keg. From what Orion had seen of Piper Garfield, he knew the cattlemen would try to fulfill a threat, even if it took the rest of the winter. Tibbs' idea had been to return Calaway's body for proper burial, then leave the accursed country. Now it seemed that Judge Yontz was going to need all the law available. Hating to leave Calaway's corpse behind. Orion concealed it under the tamarack and rode hard for Pineville.

Circling the foothills, Orion Tibbs rode north of Pineville. At the buffalo wallows he could hear desultory rifle fire, and settled down to wait for nightfall. Finally, when the sun disappeared and dusk blanketed the desert, he remounted and moved ahead until he located a Garfield sentry.

The man, stomach down on a lumpy rise, was firing liesurely into the top story of the Palace. Answering fire was high and the whine of a slug warned Orion he could become a target from both sides. He dismounted and crept forward. When his gun barrel jabbed into the back of the cowboy, the startled man turned, took one look, and slowly drew his hands away from the rifle. It took only moments for Orion to bind his captive and lead Mick on toward town. At the outskirts, he looped the reins to a mesquite bush and, staying in the shadow of an alley, finally reached Main Street. He ducked into Omar Clay's blacksmith shop. The barn seemed empty but Orion had the eerie feeling he was being watched. Remaining perfectly still, he called out. "Clay? Omar, this is Tibbs. You around . . . ?"

"Over here!" Omar's gruff voice came from the gloom. "I thought we'd seen the last of you." The blacksmith stepped forward and gave the fire in the pit a jab and suddenly grinned. "That Piper Garfield sure come huntin' for bear! Seems Newt Gobal stampeded . . ."

"I heard about that," interrupted Orion. "Where's the judge?"

"You got me, Marshal. He tried to ride out and parley with Garfield but some gun-happy cowboy shot off his hat and the judge run for cover. Ain't nobody wants to talk. Newt claims he didn't spook no herd but who'll believe that?" The big man spat. "Them two been headin' for a showdown and it's long overdue." He grimaced maliciously. " 'Course now that we got the Federal law back in town, you should settle everything right quick."

Orion had to chuckle. "It'll need an army to stop this battle. Newt's sending out for reinforcements and so is Garfield."

"Was there a lawyer in town," stated Omar, "he'd get rich makin' out wills. Time it takes any cavalry to get in here, from Fort Defiance or the Mexican border, everybody'll be dead. Tell you what; I can guess who's goin' to win." Omar waited for comment but Tibbs shook his head and Omar continued with some heat. "The first one gets in reinforcements, that's who! Something's got to break this Mexican stand-off. Garfield can't rush the town and we can't drive him off."

Orion nodded. "I'll find the judge. You stay here."

"Stay close to the buildings," warned Omar. "Them Garfield cowboys ain't real riflemen but they've got a pretty good crossfir on Main Street."

Orion had reached the door when Omar called out in an apologetic tone, "Sure glad you're back, Marshal." The sincere warmth in the smith's voice caused Orion to turn. "They're sayin' you and that Calaway was the ones who looted the stagecoach, in spite of what Emma told everybody. They also said you'd be deep in Mexico by now."

"That," Orion swore under his breath, "is where the hell I *should* be!" And ducked out the doorway.

CHAPTER TEN

Two freight wagons, high-sided and used to haul block salt, had been drawn across the street to form a barricade. The sideboards were burned and white smoke still curled around the salt blocks. A pair of horses, reins dangling, grazed in the walkway alongside the feed store. The windows of the millinery shop were broken and a dress dummy sprawled on the boardwalk. The Palace porch was still firmly in place but the railing had been yanked free and deposited in the middle of the street. The Palace windows were boarded over, the front door barricaded by upended tables.

Inside the hotel lobby and overflowing into the barroom, heavily armed men waited. The atmosphere was tense and harsh with liquor fumes and cigar smoke. The smell of exploded powder drifted down the stairs from the upper floors.

Judge Yontz and Newt Gobal had sought seclusion and moved into the small office behind the clerk's desk. The windowless room was lighted by a single coal oil lamp swinging from the low ceiling.

"Newt, you brought all this hell to Pineville!" The judge vented futile anger and waved his hand several times under Gobal's nose.

"Don't you worry, Judge." Newt was trying to stay calm. "I've got more men coming in. Then we'll nail old Garfield to the wall. Just sit back and drink your whiskey."

Yontz's voice rose. "If you'd allowed Garfield to go on his way, he'd of calmed down when I sent the marshal out. All Garfield wanted was to get Carey out of jail and his herd to winter graze. Then you . . ."

"I told you before, Judge," Newt smashed his hand onto the table, "*I* never spooked those cows!" Newt stopped hammering the table. "Both Garfield and me —we know that railroad shouldn't be brought over the pass. Ain't that so?"

Yontz nodded. "But what's that got to do with stampeding his herd?"

"I'm gettin' to that," Newt growled. "And what've we got to rile each other about? 'Course *he* says my boys rustled his cows but that's all talk. It don't hurt my feelings none 'cause I don't take him serious. So, that being the fact, why should I spook his herd?"

The judge, at a loss, spoke dully. "Somebody did it."

"They sure did. Will you keep your mind open, Judge? For just a few minutes?" Newt waited for the judge's nod. "There're only two men missing from these parts—that fellow Calaway and your man Tibbs. Right? Now, don't get into an uproar. While I talk, you think. Garfield swears there was just two men waving blankets and shootin'. Without the sudden storm, they'd 'a never been able to spook no grazin' herd. Now, who'd be right Johnny-on-the-spot when that storm come up? Tibbs and Calaway, that's who. I'm bettin' my right arm they done it!"

The judge moved around behind the table to lean against the wall. The hotelman's arguments had merit. "But why?" Judge Yontz asked weakly. "Tibbs was sent out to trail those stagecoach bandits. Calaway was acting deputy. They had no reason to do such a thing."

"There's plenty of talk," Newt said quickly, "that Tibbs could've got the railroad payroll. He could've buried it . . ."

"Don't keep harping on that!" snapped Yontz. "Mrs. Emma Clay told us Tibbs drove off the last bandit and followed them, but came back because she was left alone."

"He could've buried it," Newt repeated stubbornly. "Anyways, I don't pay no attention to Emma Clay. She always was sort of simple. Always runnin' 'way back to Kansas City to visit and she don't hardly speak to nobody." He caught himself, then went on with his case against Yontz's marshal. "Tibbs had plenty of time to hide the payroll and come back and bring in Emma Clay."

Yontz, on the defensive, protested. "What about the two stage robbers?"

"Tibbs killed them," Newt said flatly, "like he killed Roddy. He don't need no excuse for . . ."

"Lay off that!" interruped the judge. "You all know Ryan drew his gun."

Newt grinned. "So what if nobody saw him dry-gulch the two stage robbers? Let's get to my point. I say Tibbs and Calaway had a good reason for stampeding Garfield's herd. They wanted all hell to break loose. They knew Garfield would go wild; that he'd blame folks here in Pineville and start a civil war. Tibbs knew it couldn't last but it'd give them plenty of time to gather in the payroll and get across the Mexican border!"

The judge left his place by the wall to circle around and settle down in a straight-backed chair. He was nervous as a cat and Newt was pressing hard; developing a dust storm to aid his own plans. Yontz knew something of the plot percolating out of Pineville. He suspicioned Newt Gobal was fomenting surface trouble to conceal the big move. Yontz placed his palms together until the fingertips met below his chin and warned himself to keep out of Gobal's trap.

However, Newt's summary of Orion Tibbs was admittedly logical. Since the payroll robbery, rumors had been flying that Tibbs had cached the loot; that he'd returned only because of Emma Clay and had brought her in for the simple reason that he felt obligated to Omar for saving him from the "kangaroo court." Also, rumor added, Tibbs intended to ride out again when the chance presented itself. Had he, as judge, given Tibbs that chance? And wasn't Calaway, a free-booting gunslinger loosely connected with Newt Gobal, apt to join Tibbs as an accomplice?

The pair had been swallowed up. In the past two weeks there should have been some report of their activities. A drifter could have met them or a stage driver passed information along. Moreover, it did seem odd that two men could hold up a stage and completely disappear. The territory was large, but men talked and news did spread. With regret, Yontz shook his head.

Newt caught the gesture and pressed on. "Now then, Judge, whyn't you just settle this war we got going? Ride out and tell Piper Garfield what Tibbs and Calaway done to his herd. Order him to call off his cowboys and let us all get back to normal. My job's running a hotel and selling whiskey," he added plaintively, and waited for a reply. When the judge remained silent, Newt angrily continued. "You got that responsibility, Judge. If you don't take it, there's going to be plenty dead men waitin' to curse you in hell!"

"I *know* my responsibility!" Yontz straightened and barked. "I gave Tibbs three weeks and he's still got five days to go. Further," he slapped the table until the lamp oil gurgled, "I know he'll show up!"

Orion Tibbs walked up from the blacksmith shop, skirted the barricaded street corner, and entered the marshal's office. He needed time to think. This last attack by Garfield's men had been made the night before. They had been driven off. Pineville's men had withstood the charge but lacked the strength to overcome the crew of cowboys. With the possible exception of the Army, which would require days to bring in, the combatants represented the two largest forces in the territory. Roger Allan's railroaders were a third group but with little interest in Pineville's private war. And it had all been caused when he and Calaway spooked the herd.

Garfield and Newt Gobal were natural enemies. Gobal was chief of the night-owl riders and naturally Garfield had followed the arrows of suspicion in a straight line to Gobal. Tibbs clucked his dismay; he had only run the herd to get Garfield out of Pineville —to take the pressure off the judge. Now that same judge would be waiting for an explanation. Orion sat numbly in the dark office and tried to put a reasonable story together.

A full hour passed before he stepped out onto the boardwalk and closed the door. He was stepping down into the street when he suddenly halted. During this past hour, when he sought in vain for an excuse, he hadn't once considered the easy way out; simply to saddle up Mick and ride out of Pineville.

Orion, recalling the sentry he had left tied near the buffalo wallows, was glad that the angle of the back balcony prevented vagrant gunfire. He edged to the door of Yontz's room and rapped. A moment passed before slippered feet reached the door and a low voice asked, "Is that you, Judge?"

Orion recognized Peggy's contralto and barked, "It's Tibbs. I'm looking for the judge."

"He's downstairs with Newt." She sounded defiant. "He told me to meet him here."

"That's being a real good, obedient girl," Orion said testily and stalked away.

He found Judge Yontz and Newt Gobal still together in the office. Gobal was surprised and sullenly angry. Yontz smiled slightly, and taking the marshal by the elbow, led the way from the office. They found chairs in a corner of the lobby and Yontz settled back. "Calaway come back with you?" he asked.

Orion shook his head. "He's dead. I left him in the brush near the foot of Crater Pass."

"Oh . . . ?" It caught the judge with a lighted match halfway to his cigar.

"He died of gangrene," Orion added.

"Bullet wound?" At Tibbs' nod, the judge continued slowly. "Dangerous country. Lots of ways a man can get hurt."

Orion Tibbs reached to lift the burning match from Yontz's fingers, dropped the glowing stick into a cuspidor and searched his vest pocket for another match which he held to the cigar tip. He shrugged. "Calaway was shot the night we spooked Garfield's herd. He died two weeks later."

Yontz bit into the cigar to hide his ripple of shock. "Where?"

"At a hunter's old hideout on the rimrock. We thought he could beat it but the poison got to him. He died yesterday. I was bringing his body back when I learned there was a small civil war going on around here."

"You had some reason for stampeding that herd?" the judge asked hollowly, but with hope underlying his tone.

Orion nodded, knowing his answer was lame. "I figured it would suck Garfield out of Pineville. Give things a chance to calm down."

"I'll accept that for now," the judge said simply. He exhaled and added, "We'll have to ride out and face Garfield."

Orion nodded and rose but Yontz waved toward the stairway. "Not tonight. Get some sleep, Marshal. We'll save it till morning." As Orion started up the stairs, Yontz called after him, "I'm glad you came back, Marshal."

Orion Tibbs nodded with some satisfaction. Well, he thought, that made two men—Omar Clay and the judge—glad to have him back. Maybe he was gaining?

CHAPTER ELEVEN

It dawned cold. Frost sparkled on the ground and lay ice crystals on the green sage. The rain puddles had soaked into the ground, making it hard and cold. Orion Tibbs and Judge Yontz, bundled in mackinaws and wearing sheepskin gloves, rode out to Garfield's camp. Yontz had tied a white scarf onto a willow stick and it fluttered in the chilling wind.

Orion, watching Mick's breath vaporize, wondered exactly what the judge intended to do. Playing it safe, Orion had slipped the riot guns into his saddlebags and had also hidden a four-shot Derringer in his boot top. If Piper Garfield exploded and decided to take his revenge on the spot, Orion wanted to be ready.

Garfield's command post was established in the old adobe. He had brought in his cookwagon and the cook had a sputtering coffee pot dangling above the campfire. The cook saw their approach and alerted the camp. By the time Orion and the judge reached the broken wall half a dozen rifles were trained in their direction.

"Tell Garfield we're here," Yontz ordered. "That we're here to put a quick end to this insanity."

Piper Garfield swaggered out of the adobe and

faced the pair from town. "I heard that, Judge. Suppose you explain. If that damned Newt Gobal—or any of his lying cattle rustlers—thinks he's going to get off this hook, he's damned badly mistaken! 'Fore we're through, we're going to hang some hides to dry and run every outlaw outa Arizona territory."

Staring coldly around, Yontz ignored the threat. "We didn't come out here to talk facing guns! Tell your men to back off so we can talk plain."

"You'd better get down and come into my office," Garfield snapped, ordering the cook to bring in coffee. He led the way, pushing aside a blanket covering the empty door frame. The adobe was full of gear and the cattleman kicked a space clear, then waved a hand to indicate the parley was open.

"There are still PG cattle on the high ridges," Yontz said. "You going to bunk here until the snow catches them?"

"They can wait," muttered Garfield. "It won't take long before more men come in. Then . . ."

Yontz quickly countered. "Newt Gobal says the same thing. So you're both building up forces and it'll come to a stand-off with lots of killing. Is that what you want, Piper?"

"You should talk, Judge!" Garfield retorted with a hot glance at Orion. "This gun-slinging U.S. Marshal you dredged out of Yuma Prison has already killed Roddy Ryan and gunned down Carey. *He* started this fight."

"And he's the Federal lawman in this section," Yontz boldly retorted, "so let's leave the law enforcing in his hands. Any complaints you or Newt Gobal have to make can go through the courts. You can attack Pineville again—and maybe overrun the town—but that's when you'll find your troubles are only beginning. You'll face murder charges for every man who dies. There are soldiers at Tucson and all along the border. They'll be used to support the court. You hear me, Garfield?"

The cook entered with three steaming cups and passed them around. He took a speculative look at the three taut men and waited. Garfield, lips gulping the steaming liquid, glared at the marshal. He swallowed, then spoke. "The judge has a lot of guts, bringing you out here. I've got ten men outside who would give you time to draw—and still outshoot you." His voice and temper rose. "Might just be able to do it myself! Carey was drunk when you manhandled him . . ." The cook grunted assent and Garfield shouted, "Get on outside, Jake!"

Orion held his temper. The judge was doing fine. If Garfield still had cattle above the snow line he would have to find a quick settlement of this battle. While his cowboys were laying siege to Pineville, those cattle would suffer in the early snow and, as snow blocked the passes, would die. The judge had hit home with his murder charges. Garfield's stake was permanent; he couldn't risk his holdings with a mass killing. He would have to face the Territorial courts. The small room grew explosive with Garfield's frustrating dilemma and the worst was yet to come. Yontz would be admitting that his own marshal had stampeded the herd. Could Garfield take that? He'd already lost face when he was unable to bluff Carey out of jail and had been driven back from his abortive attempt to overrun Pineville. Yontz would have to come up with something to give Garfield a chance to back off from his position without losing face. Orion decided to let Yontz play out his string, yet he flinched as the judge continued.

"Newt Gobal never spooked your herd, Garfield." Yontz nodded in Orion's direction, speaking with quiet force. "You're looking at the man who did."

It took Garfield by surprise. Dark blood rose in his chunky face as he stared at the judge. "*He* did?" he asked in a squeak. "The marshal did *that?* Scattered a man's cows all over hell's half-acre? And you got the gumption to *tell me?*"

"That's right," Yontz calmly replied, but avoided a direct answer to the astonished question. "I'd say right now you're financially responsible for any damage Pineville's suffered. When Carey wrecked Raphael's Cantina, you paid for the damages and so it will be with the damage to Pineville. It could cost you plenty . . ."

Garfield ignored the judge's legal point. "Why'd he spook my herd?" he demanded. "Ain't no law says . . ."

"The marshal has a pretty fair argument," Yontz went on, his voice patient. "Look at the facts. You're a very powerful man, Piper, with fifty rifles to back up your threats. You demanded the release of a prisoner and threatened to kill the marshal, right?"

Garfield, as though completely intrigued in a stunned sort of way by the judge's legal discourse, nodded.

"This marshal could expect no support from the local citizens. He had no authority to order you out of town. He certainly could not surrender his prisoner. So what could he do? Why, he could have killed you." The judge paused and pursed his lips. "But he did not. Instead he stampeded your herd, knowing that would draw you and all your men out of Pineville. I would say that any court would uphold his judgment."

Garfield's mouth was hanging open and the judge, with sonorous judicial inflection, continued. "Now, who can justify the marshal's behavior? The courts. However, before his act can be judged, we must have a complaint. When you file such a complaint, I'm sure the counter complaint will be filed that claims damages for destruction in and about Pineville. One word to Newt Gobal, and he'll be delighted to file such damages."

"There were two of them!" blurted Piper Garfield.

The judge nodded. "His deputy."

Silence deepened in the room. Garfield, caught on the dilemma hoisted by the judge, squirmed. Finally, muttering, he leaped up and strode outside. His shouted orders to break camp drifted into the room. Judge Yontz cocked his head at the resultant sounds of feverish activity, then turned and winked solemnly at the marshal.

They waited. Several minutes passed before Piper

Garfield returned. The action outside had given him time to gather his wits and his next threat was a cold statement of endurance. "A man can take a lot but . . ." He edged up to Orion and snapped, "Twice now, you've twisted my tail. I've even lost face with my cook. Don't do it again. Now, get the hell out of here. I don't want you in my house!"

They buried Calaway the following day. The Pineville graveyard was a fenced-in knob, covered with mesquite sage and sandy gravel. The dirt shoveled from the grave was fresh and lay red in the sun. The opening yawned in the shade of exposed dirt. A few of the graves were marked by stones or wooden crosses. The older ones were marked by wheel hubs and broken buffalo skulls. Several plots were fenced off with wrought iron that attested to the professional skill of the blacksmith. The road leading into the graveyard was rutty, and Omar Clay's funeral wagon rocked until Orion climbed up to steady the board coffin.

They unloaded the coffin beside the grave, and when they straightened, both looked back toward town. One carriage approached. Orion recognized the judge's team. They were pulling a two-seater carriage and Peggy Smith was sitting up front with the judge.

"It seems nobody cares much," Omar stated, "but it's nice the judge could come out. He can say a few words. Sometimes the Palace girls help bury them, but this time it looks like Peggy Smith is the only one."

"Only because the judge came," grunted Orion, in such a bitter tone the blacksmith dropped the subject.

Judge Yontz reined in, backed his rig into the shade of the fence, and helped Peggy down. Her white skirt was long and she gathered several folds of the cloth together to keep the hem out of the sand. She wore a green blouse but no jewelry. Her shining hair was tucked into a matching green bonnet with a strip of lace around the brim. Peggy walked forward as Yontz followed, and they nodded to Orion and Omar.

"I never knew Calaway," the judge remarked, and turned to Orion. "What kind of a man was he?"

"Like the rest," answered Orion. "A fellow who could use a gun, a real expert on a horse. Which," he added, "seems odd as he came from Ireland."

"That's a pretty good description," Yontz nodded. "A hard-riding Irishman who could use a gun. I expect he was religious, so we'll say a prayer for his soul." He moved to the graveside and motioned the others to join him. "We are joined here this afternoon to ask . . ."

Peggy Smith halted him by placing a hand on his arm and he turned as she motioned toward the cemetery road. A dozen horsemen, escorting a fringed surrey filled with the ladies from the Palace, had left the outskirts and were nearing the cemetery. Peggy smiled. "More of Calaway's friends?" she asked.

Orion nodded. Their arrival would help reduce the gloom by a show of respect for the dead man.

This interment on a lonely hump in a vast, boundless land, with only four people present, had been disturbing. Death rode a sluggish horse when he gunned Calaway. The weeks of pain in the cabin, the ride back with the corpse, interrupted by Garfield's attack on the town, had extracted a strain. More mourners, Orion thought, would indeed be welcome.

Newt Gobal was leading the procession. He dismounted and strode back to aid the ladies over ruts to the grave, and the graveyard seemed to come alive when he shouted, "Now, you all better mind your manners! We'll gather 'round and put old Calaway away proper. Now, ladies, let the judge up front. I declare, he's the only person present who knows the right words, but we can all say 'Amen.' Will you proceed, Judge?"

"Would anyone know the deceased's given name?" asked Yontz.

The Palace group consulted together but turned back with blank faces. Newt Gobal broke the silence. "Most everyone knew him, called him Cal." Newt drew his Colt and added, "Let's send him off with a salute to Cal Calaway." He hammered a slug into the sky. Orion caught himself pulling back to reach for his gun as the men whooped and emptied their pistols in a shattering volley. Somewhat sheepishly, Omar and Orion joined. With the firing over, Judge Yontz advised those present to bow their heads. He sang out a few Bible quotes and the funeral was over.

Newt Gobal, being genial for a purpose, waited until the mourners moved away before he spoke to

Orion. "Garfield," he said, "pulled out quick. I figured maybe it had something to do with Calaway's being killed?"

Orion nodded, noncommittally. "Just might have."

Newt, discovering the conversation was over, rejoined his group and led them back to town. The judge helped Peggy Smith into his rig and drove off with a wave.

On the ride back in Omar's wagon, Orion asked, "Why do you suppose Newt showed up?"

"He never attended no funerals before," mused the blacksmith. "An' did you notice he had the better part of the local hoot-owls with him? You figure they was up to something?"

"Could be," admitted the puzzled marshal.

"But wasn't it all sort of nice?" Omar smiled with somber satisfaction, smacking the whip against the team's rumps. "Funerals is generally pretty solemn. You know, the corpse shiverin' in the damp ground an' all? Little excitement sorta warms a body up."

Orion Tibbs nodded but couldn't shake the feeling something even more exciting was about to happen.

CHAPTER TWELVE

A knocking on the thin door panel seeped through Orion's deep sleep and he fumbled groggily for his gunbelt. The rapping increased until he called out, "Who's there?"

The muffled voice of Judge Yontz answered and the pounding began again, continuing while Orion left the bed and walked across the room. The judge was spacing his pounding with impatient shouts. "This is Yontz! Wake up and open this fool door. We've got some real trouble at Crater Pass!"

The judge paced the floor while Orion was dressing. A message from Roger Allan, brought in by a weary rider, had urgently requested the presence of the marshal at the site of construction. The Crater Pass tunnel had been blown up; heavy charges of black powder had closed both openings and tunnel workers were trapped. According to the messenger's information, ten men had died and at least seven more were trapped in the cave-in. Rescue work was proceeding, but Roger Allan was boiling mad and demanding that the law respond and capture the blasters.

Yontz, as he stormed about the room, was vengefully dejected. "This is the last straw!" He yelled. "The railroad people have sunk their bankroll on that short route. That tunnel *has* to come through."

"Some delay, maybe." Orion tried to pacify Yontz, avoiding the pacing man long enough to struggle into a sheepskin coat.

"Delay?" Yontz flailed his arms. "Nothing of the kind. It's total disaster! That rider said the entire face of the mountain came down. To get through that route now, they'd have to trestle better'n two miles along a crumbling cliff. He said—Roger Allan said . . ."

"Maybe there's another way, Judge?" Orion interpolated.

Yontz exploded, waving both arms. "Allan was the engineer who laid out the route. Wouldn't *he* know if there was another way?"

"So the railroad gambled and the gamble didn't pay off."

"They laid out a safe route. Who'd expect someone—out of meanness—to blow up a tunnel? What we're going to have around here is just another hole-in-the-wall. There just isn't any hope for this country! Newt Gobal's got himself a robber's roost. Every bandit in the West can lay out here. Garfield will get his cattle shipping terminal at Rail Head—a water hole in the desert. That's all," he ranted on, "it will ever amount to. Shipping pens on a side track! This country, with all its potential, will stay closed until doomsday."

Orion quieted a sudden desire to add that trouble follows trouble. Blasting the Crater Pass Tunnel was serious, but there was something else brewing which could explode the territory and even shake Washington. Calaway had warned that Newt was up to something tremendous—"The Big Raid" the dead man had called it. However, the judge was too wound up to take any more so Orion Tibbs brushed silently past, left the room and headed for the livery stable.

The scene at the cave-in was chaotic. The face of Crater Pass, where a ridge had risen straight and clean, was now crumbled. Chunks of fire-twisted stone were cascaded into the mouth of the pass. A sagging lip, where the tunnel exited, flared inward. Above, where the mountain sloped away, was a straight face of pure rock.

Orion crossed the crater meadow and guided Mick up the boulder-strewn road to the headquarters shack. Men with brush skill were burrowing into the debris. Rails were being laid and timbers hustled into the dusty maw. Hose lines, throbbing with steam, followed the rails and threshing machinery echoed.

Roger Allan waved Orion into the shack. The engineer was pale with weariness but his words rasped with anger. "Who ever arranged this blast . . ." He shook his head and gritted his teeth. "I want them caught, Tibbs—I want them hung!"

"You know who did this?" Orion asked.

"Newt Gobal, that's who!" Allan's words were coated with revulsion.

"Did you see him . . . ?" began Orion, then quickly explained. "I'm not a detective but we'll need more than just a close guess to arrange any hanging for Newt Gobal."

"Gobal didn't want this road to come through!" shouted Allan. "He fixed that for sure," he went on bitterly. "The management will pull back. They'll circle and"—vacantly, he stared at the wall as he prophesied—"the vast, potential market will escape. We'll just lay rails through the sand to haul cattle. The mines, without transportation for ore, and the mills and forests will lay dormant."

"Let me say this." Orion caught Roger Allan's attention then continued his thought. "Garfield just might be the one who ordered the blasting. He's had some terrible experiences happen to him in the high country and he's been a mighty violent man when riled."

"If you believe that, why aren't you after him?"

Orion raised a hand to calm the angry man. "I'll need something to go on. You see any of Garfield's men around?"

Roger Allan shook his head. "*I* think it's Newt Gobal. You say Piper Garfield. All I want . . ."

"Is to string them up?" interrupted Orion with an inward smile. When someone suffered a hurt they always wanted a victim—someone whose suffering would act as a poultice to heal their own wound. He had been such a victim and had wallowed in the hell that was Territorial Prison. He wondered if the dead banker or the bank depositors had felt better. If Roger Allan's fury was generated by the death of his tunnel men, it would be easier to understand.

"That's *right!*" Allan's wrath broke through Orion's whimsical thoughts. "Just get the man responsible. Hanging's too good!"

"You have a scout?" Orion asked. "Someone who knows the line? Knows where you store the explosives and . . ."

"Peel," Allan quickly inserted. "Sidney Peel. The fellows call him 'Buffalo.' He was with us on the survey and now he brings in the meat for the commissary."

"We'll backtrack and maybe find something. Where'll I find him?"

"Up with the track-layers," Roger Allan snapped. "We have a cook car back there and Peel's working out of that spot." He waved a hand and Orion left.

The marshal located the commissary car two miles below the tunnel. A hundred feet of siding angled off from the line and the commissary car—a battered boxcar with narrow windows—squatted in the middle of a dozen tents. Orion found Peel seated at the cook's table playing solitaire. He was dressed as a frontiersman; buckskin jacket of doubtful vintage with fringed sleeves worn through at both elbows. His hair, almost long enough to braid, flowed over the collar of the jacket. Peel's face was lined but ageless, the cheekbones sharp and the nose pointed. His mouth was wide and his strong teeth stained by chewing tobacco. He wore blue Army pants tucked into fine Mexican boots.

"You're Buffalo Peel?" Orion asked as he slid into a barrel chair and faced the scout.

"Peel, all right, but don't call me Buffalo. My name's Sid, Sid Peel. You're . . . ?"

"Tibbs, U.S. Marshal," answered Orion. "Roger Allan said you were a scout for the survey. Thought you and I might do some backtracking."

Peel studied his cards and began gathering them into a pile. "Meat supply is up. Could waste a couple days, if'n it's what the boss wants. You the convict," he looked up, "Judge Yontz sprung from Territorial?"

"You guessed it," smiled Orion.

Without haste, Sid Peel arranged with a fat cook for a sack of trail supplies, and in half an hour led the way over the rim behind the Crater Pass cut.

"They coulda come from two directions." Peel eased his horse along the hogback and reined in. "Over there from Pineville"—he pointed north—"or, of course, from the south—cattle country. One thing for sure—they had to have at least four men."

"Four men would leave quite a trail," mused Orion, a question underlying the remark.

"Had to be at least four," repeated Sid Peel. "It took a good four barrels of powder to blow that tunnel. Had to be made in one trip. And the fuse a mighty long one so's they could get away."

"A man working with the crew could've lighted a short fuse," objected Orion.

"Argumentative, ain't you, Tibbs?"

"Touchy, ain't you, Sid?"

"One tunnel man'd never bury another one.

They're pretty close. Had to be someone from outside."

"A track man for a few bucks of easy money?"

"That might be true," nodded Peel. "We got some awful riffraff. An' with paydays bein' so far apart they just might be soreheaded riffraff."

"Afraid they won't get their wages?" Orion asked.

"There's talk that the railroad is mighty near broke. Some's gettin' worried," admitted Peel. "Then there's the others . . ."

"Others?" Orion asked then suddenly guessed. "Gunslingers?"

Sid Peel spat into the top of a bush. "Drifters, Army deserters and such. Some mixed breeds. Most never seen a crowbar. In spite of bein' warned, Allan takes them on."

"Would they blow up the tunnel?" Orion probed.

"Might, if they wasn't gettin' paid right on time. Railroad pay has been mighty slow," complained the meat hunter. "Man's gotta pay cash for whiskey."

"Seems the railroad could be using Pinkertons," offered Orion.

"They'd be afraid to get off the right of way." Peel was scornful. "We got men who eat detectives for breakfast."

Orion reined Mick's stubby head around and stroked the thick mane. Chancing a rebuff, he asked the querulous Peel a question. "Many men around drawing pay while waiting for the big raid?"

"Expect so." Peel gave Orion a quizzical look before adding, "You figure they got orders to slow down the construction?"

"Could be," Orion said and, thinking out loud, spelled it out. "The men blowing the tunnel must belong to the crew. Who else would know how to steal the powder or have an opportunity to place the charges?"

"So what'll we find up here?" Peel's tone was ironical. "The blasters've gotta be in camp. Hadn't we better go back?"

Nodding, Orion reined around. With Sid Peel following in a bouncy gallop, they headed back to the railroad camp.

CHAPTER THIRTEEN

Orion spent the early afternoon in close contact with the track crew. The construction company had recruited work gangs from the east. Eastern derbies, stained brown by weather, were common. The twang of the Middle West mingled with soft Gaelic. Dutchmen from Pennsylvania sang their guttural songs and drove spikes with measured strokes. The grunting men, in sweaty red undershirts and cobbled boots, were hammering a railbed through the defiant Tooloons.

Others—Orion estimated about one-to-five—were lean Westerners. These favored big hats and pointed boots, belted jeans, stained by gunbelt shadows, and tight shirts. Leather vests flapped over chests made waspish from hauling on cutting ropes.

The marshal paid particular attention to the latter type. A few he recognized as habitues of Newt Gobal's Palace Bar. They raised slanty eyebrows to throw flinty glares as the marshal stared at first one, then another.

One man, openly defiant, glared back. He was a 'breed called Yolo, with a thin frame supporting a broad, round Shoshone head. He carried a Bowie knife in a doeskin scabbard braided onto his sixgun holster. His arrogant posture indicated he considered himself an expert with either weapon. Orion remembered him from the vigilante meeting. The man had made several close passes with the butt of a broken whiskey bottle. It also could be that Yolo was recalling the three days he had spent in Orion's crowded jail. Orion got the feeling the belligerent glare was fused now with a sliver of fear.

For a full hour Orion sat on the steep bank above the crew and studied Yolo. As the man grew more nervous, Orion's feeling grew more positive that Yolo was involved in the tunnel explosion. If he could force Yolo's hand now, the man could make a mistake.

When the sun dropped, long shadows from the mountains fell over the construction site. Men gathered coats and lunch pails, and lighted pipes and twirlies as they waited for the work train.

Orion remained close to Yolo. When the engine shuttled two flatcars up the grade and he was sure Yolo was aboard, he mounted Mick and headed for the camp.

Sid Peel was waiting at the cook car. He nodded briefly to Orion who stepped close, dropping his voice. "Find any suspects?"

Peel nodded. "Three. You?"

"Yes, one." Orion reversed a step and spoke in a normal tone. "Where do they line up for supper?"

"There . . ." Peel pointed. A full barrel of hard cookies was stacked by the rear of the cook-car. "The cook keeps them waiting," he explained. "They'll fill up on those. Cookies are cheap."

"When they all get here," Orion again lowered his voice, "we'll walk right in. Let me do the talking. Yolo will have to jump me or bolt. Either way, we'll use him."

"He one of the blasters?" Peel asked, puzzled. "You wanted me to pick out the three toughest critters on the work gang but that don't say they did the blasting."

"If we're right about the railroad men doing the blasting, then one or all four could be guilty. You see the three you picked?"

Peel nodded as he stared over the group of men. "I see them and they've all got a gun buckled on," he added morosely. "They come ready for a showdown. I been tellin' everyone you was going to pick the tunnel blasters out of the gang during supper call. Them that did it couldn't run, so maybe they come for a shoot-out!"

Orion nodded. "Yolo's our key. He's got to make the first move. You take a position on the high bank where you can look down on everyone." Sid Peel nodded and moved off.

Mounting the rear platform, Orion gazed out until the men stopped shifting around. He knew he had a tiger by the tail. If Yolo remained stolid and the three men Sid Peel had pointed out kept their heads, he could be laughed out of camp. This was a high-stakes game and a poor bluff would send a person into the discard.

Suddenly, Orion pointed a rigid finger at Yolo and shouted, "Step back away from that man!" He waited a few seconds until the crowd began to shift and again shouted, "There were ten men killed when he blew up the Crater Pass Tunnel!" The men, startled by the marshal's blunt words, threw a covert glance at Yolo and waited for Orion to go on.

"There're seven more men buried under those big lava rocks. *I* say Yolo lugged four barrels of powder into that tunnel and, for a few dirty bucks, killed those ten men!" He held up a hand, flat palm out. "But, I'm not going to allow any lynching here. I'm taking him back to Pineville to stand trial."

Yolo stepped forward, legs stiffened by nervousness, and glared up at Orion Tibbs. His thick lips were drawn back from yellowed teeth, his voice grim with fury as he shouted, "All day long you been staring down my neck!" He raised a shaking fist to punctuate his denial. "What right you got tellin' what you're going to do—sayin' that we blasted the tunnel? You better prove that, Marshal, 'cause if you don't, we'll make you eat that gun!"

Orion smiled as he heard the soft curse from the back of the crowd. Men had begun to edge away from Yolo. Orion leaned out over the railing and brought the accusing finger directly in front of Yolo's flushed face. "*We*, Yolo? Are you saying you didn't do the job alone? I figured you were too damned stupid. Were those three with the holsters tied down helping you?"

Yolo jerked around to stare. The three gunmen gaped back. Orion was silent, letting an ominous quiet gather, then Yolo began to fidget. His eyes widened as he realized he had indicted the others. The front gunfighter cursed as he went for his gun.

The hurried shot missed and the slug sang over Orion's head as he leaped clear of the platform. The chow line broke and confused men dodged from the line of fire. The single shot had opened a line like a furrow between Orion and his quarry. Yolo, still braced solidly, was bringing up his Colt.

Orion Tibbs, moving to the right in a low crouch to keep Yolo in the line of fire, triggered two shots past the man. Before the bemused Yolo could aim, Orion shot. Yolo's compadres were drawn together and firing in desperation. Sid Peel stuck his head over the bank and triggered rapid rifle shots into the threesome.

A convulsive scream, followed by the clatter of a fallen six-gun, ended the shooting. Orion, stalking past Yolo's body, approached his victims. Sid Peel, ejecting a spent shell from a smoking Winchester, joined Orion.

Two of the men were down, crumpled in death. The third, his gun hand bloody and face contorted, was the screamer. Looking up from his crippled hand, he began yelling, "That crazy breed! I hope to hell he's dead. He's too stupid to live!"

"Not as stupid as you," retorted Orion.

"What's that?"

"You were working for him," answered Orion.

"Yolo's dead," stated Sid Peel. With respect for Orion's aim, he went on, "Plugged right through the cowlick!" He nudged the two forms with his rifle muzzle. "So's these two. Over the hill and very dead. That one," he pointed, "was named Cash."

"That takes care of the blasters." Orion felt he had discharged the duties expected of a lawman. "We'd better rush this wounded one out of here before there's a lynching." He was disappointed that Yolo had died. Yontz might have been able to tie Newt Gobal and Yolo together. Cash claimed he was working for Yolo, yet who could accept that? However, Cash might be able to implicate Newt.

The scout broke into his thoughts. "Walk Cash back to the corral. Saddle up and take him out, right quick. I'll see the other corpses are brought in a buckboard."

Orion turned to his prisoner. "You ever work for Newt Gobal?"

"No."

"Then why'd you blow up the tunnel?"

"Yolo paid out the money," Cash answered sullenly. "He never said who give it to him."

"You know Newt Gobal?"

"I heard of him."

"Were you joining the big raid?"

"I ain't sayin' . . ." He looked around nervously. "Didn't you say we better get out of here pretty quick?"

Orion shrugged. "If you talk, I'll hurry."

Cash turned worried eyes toward the railroad men who were beginning to regroup. Quickly he nodded

assent, then pleaded, "Can we get this hand ban-
daged and on the road first?"

"I guess we had better," Orion agreed.

They made camp an hour after sundown. It had
been a long eighteen hours since Judge Yontz had
pounded on his hotel door to announce the tunnel
blast at Crater Pass. Now, two hours out of the railroad camp and deep in protective brush, Orion felt it
would be safe to rest for the night. His wounded prisoner had been complaining and Mick was beginning
to tire. Somewhere behind, Sid Peel would be on his
way into Pineville with the three dead men.

The night had turned cold and a quickening wind
tore at the undergrowth. Orion built a fire against a
rock wall that served as a heat reflector. He took another look at Cash's wound. The man was suffering
and glad to be off the jolting horse. "No coffee?" he
asked querulously.

"Nope. Just a fire and a place out of the wind. Tomorrow we'll have you safe in jail." Orion rolled a
smoke, passed it to Cash, and hunkered down against
the wall. "The big raid, Cash? Time to talk."

The prisoner took a deep drag and feigned surprise. "You really don't know?"

"Some. Start talking."

"It's the biggest thing ever to hit the territory,"
Cash began boastfully. "A clean sweep from here to
the border."

"Cattle?"

"From south of the Tooloons clear to the Mexican
border."

"Whyn't you start at the beginning?" Orion asked, curbing his impatience.

"You were in Territorial Prison," Cash was brusk. "You musta heard about it." He noticed Orion's rising anger and hurriedly added, "All right, so you don't know. Then listen . . ." They were his last two words.

Orion saw the flame shooting from the bushwhacker's rifle before he heard the gunfire. The slug caught him across the temple and slanted down to rip away part of his cheek. He rose, his head full of roaring echoes, and caught a fleeting glance of the crafty smile on Cash's face. Orion stumbled and the second shot missed. He felt the world turning and went down on wobbling knees. Cash caught him with a kick which threw Orion completely off balance and he fell, shoulder first, against the rock wall and began a desperate roll toward the undergrowth.

Cash, on his feet, was following the downed marshal and kicking viciously. Orion reached up and dragged his attacker down. He was now deep in the brush and crawling, but the rifleman continued to rake the area. Orion lay still, trying to gather strength to burrow deeper. He listened. A pair of bootheels were dragging against the rock. Another man was shouting directions from higher up. "To the right! To the right! He went into the brush. Damn it, man, get in there after him!"

"He ain't dead!" was the wary reply. "An' he's still wearin' his gun belt."

"I'll cover you. Go on in there, he's wounded!"

"Come on down an' go in yourself!" the other man snarled.

"Where's Cash?"

"He's dead an' I'm gettin' out!"

Orion, face pressed into the dirt, heard the boots retreat. He pushed out with a wobbly arm but couldn't rise. His head felt like a balloon and his eyes burned. He tried to reach his holster and pain tore through his jaw. He pushed with his feet and felt himself begin to slide on the pine needles. Finally, he was able to roll over and locate the campfire. Cash was sprawled like a broken sack of oats. After what seemed like an eternity, he was able to work his elbows under himself and start a torturous crawl deeper into the protective brush.

CHAPTER FOURTEEN

Sid Peel drove the light wagon into Pineville, tied the reins to the footbrake and leaned back to straighten the stained canvas. He shook his head and climbed down. A fat man stared down from the porch and Peel asked, "Is there a Judge Yontz here?"

"Mostly he can be found in the barroom. Want I should see?"

"Ask him to step out here," Sid Peel directed. "Then maybe you could round up your doctor?"

In minutes the fat man returned with the judge, then, nodding to Peel, scurried up the street toward Dr. Saber's office.

The scout directed the judge to approach the wagon. With a slow hand he raised the canvas and stepped aside. The judge's face was a study as he turned. "Five bodies? The men who died in the tunnel blast?"

"Four of them are the tunnel blasters and the fifth is your marshal, Tibbs, but he ain't dead—quite yet. I'll tell you how it must've all come about . . ."

"Later!" snapped the judge. "If he's alive, we'd better get him inside."

An hour later, Dr. Saber was still working over Orion's unconscious form. Sid Peel and Judge Yontz had adjourned to the balcony with a bottle and two glasses.

Peel filled in Yontz on the graphic details of the shooting near the cook-car, then ended lamely, "I don't know what really happened to the marshal. He'd crawled down to the road and that's where I found him. He was pretty bad. With that jaw wound, he ain't been able to say a word. I backtracked some and found this Cash fellow's body. There had to be two bushwhackers. They cut down on Tibbs but was afraid to go into the brush after him and skedaddled." He shook his head sadly. "An' we thought them blasters was stupid!"

"How's that?" asked the judge.

" 'Cause the marshal only figured there was four of them who done it. You see?"

The judge paused to pour drinks. He pushed a brimming glass to Peel and slowly asked, "You drink this one real slow, then you might tell me why Tibbs was so stupid?"

The scout lifted the drink, sniffed the aroma, smiled and drank carefully. Setting down the glass, he repeated, "We figured they was only four blasters, understand? Actually, there was at least six—Yolo, his three partners, and the two who ambushed the marshal. Them last two never made their move when Yolo caved in. They just waited and followed the marshal. He was a sittin' duck. You understand, Judge?"

Yontz sipped his drink and changed the subject. "What's going to happen up there on the railroad?"

Sid Peel groaned. "Them directors of Roger Allan's are commercial cannibals. They'll back down off'n that mountain with all skids greased. You better figure the north slope of the Tooloons is forever lost to civilization. Cattle will be king. Garfield and the rest will cover Arizona with meat frames until even the prairie dogs will starve."

"Garfield wanted it that way," mused the judge. "Could he have hired those men to wreck the Crater Pass tunnel?"

"He could have," Sid Peel answered, "but that don't quite fit Garfield. You can't horse with his property, nor his rights, else you got a fight on your hands. He's ornery as a boozed-up Apache, but he'll come straight down the road to spit in your eye. I don't picture Piper Garfield hirin' killers."

"There's Roger Allan's crew . . ." Yontz skirted the question which had to bring Newt Gobal flush into the picture.

"Mosta them are plain workin' stiffs," Sid Peel stated and when Yontz remained silent, he elaborated. "They work hard, eat heavy and drink when they can get their pay. Some owes plenty at the saloon tents. They ain't killers—not the kind would wreck their own tunnel and kill other tunnel men. Except . . ." Sid was silent so long the judge broke the silence impatiently.

"Except what? You forget that at least four of the work crew had to be gunned down and . . ."

"Yolo and them others was fresh on the job," barked the scout. "They was real, hired cutthroats.

They done it damned good but had to stick around for a bit. If they'd run, everyone'd know who done it, see? Tibbs showed up before they could ease out. He tricked that stupid Yolo . . ." Peel broke off and stared quizzically into Judge Yontz's heavy lidded eyes. "Judge, we all know who done the blastin' and we all know who paid for the job. You expectin' to get something outa this bottle?" Peel's long fingers caressed the glass of red liquor as he demanded, "You expect something that'll let Newt Gobal off the hook?"

Yontz's face flushed in resentment at Peel's deliberate slur and he replied in a half-shout. "There isn't any way to prove Gobal arranged or paid for it!"

Peel's snort crackled with cynical amusement. "Same with Garfield, same with Gobal? Then who ordered it done and paid the blood money? Maybe the railroad commissioners? Maybe the Apaches? Maybe the Mexicans, or even the trappers in the Tooloons?"

"They all have an axe to grind," Yontz said tersely, "even your railroad crew. The workers, like yourself, haven't been paid for two months. Supposing they wanted a little revenge, something to hurry the wages along?"

Peel's answer crackled like a bullwhip. "I heard all about you and Tibbs! You got him out of prison so's he could scare off or gun down the wild ones, 'ceptin' Tibbs was a mite more man than you bargained for. He's pickin' on your pets. He throwed Newt Gobal in jail; he run Garfield outa Pineville. Then he went up onto the railroad and caught the ones needed catching. And now he's maybe dyin' for doing what a marshal's supposed to do. And you're sittin' here trying to protect Gobal!"

"What? *Me* protect Newt Gobal?" Yontz shoved his jaw forward, but Sid Peel went right on.

"I'll put it this way, Judge." Peel sounded ready to spit like a cobra. "Your beanbag kind of law ain't ready for the territory or the territory ain't ready for it! Tibbs' kind, that's what this country understands. Tibbs and his six-gun law. You just turn that man loose on Newt Gobal, and *then* you'll have peace and safety . . ."

"Without proof?" Yontz reared back. "Why, no jury'd convict . . ."

Peel interrupted, his voice slick with sarcasm. "And when you gonna get your proof? After the big . . .?" In disgust, the scout closed his lips with a snap and rose from the chair.

"What the hell do you know?" asked Yontz. Peel, his soft moccasins noiseless against the floor, turned back with a scowl as Judge Yontz again shouted, "And just where the hell are you going?"

"I'm going to look in on Tibbs," was the growled response. "With friends like you, the marshal don't need no enemies. After that, I'm going to find me a gravedigger and we're going to bury them four men still in the wagon."

The judge slipped lower in his chair and watched the pugnacious scout stride toward the door. Lifting a dejected hand, the judge quietly offered, "Take them down to Omar Clay's. He does all the burying around here."

Orion Tibbs' sickroom was hot and smelled of liniment. Sid Peel stepped into the room. His face softened as he watched Dr. Saber fluff a pillow and ease it under the marshal's limp head. A yard away, at a bench-like table, Peggy Smith was wringing out a cloth in a white washbowl. The water was stained with blood. When she lifted her head to nod at Sid, he noticed the compassion in the luminous green eyes and nodded back.

"How about the marshal, Doc?" Sid asked. "Can he make it?"

"Some do, some don't." Dr. Saber's reply was without inflection but carried a resolve which reassured Sid Peel. "Head wounds are touchy. The slug never penetrated the bone, yet God knows what it shook loose inside his skull." He talked on like he wanted the two people in the room to understand he was qualified to help the marshal. "A slug—a rifle slug— tears a pretty big hole. He must have had his mouth open or he'd have lost the jawbone. The bullet was fired from above him. It cut across the temple and projected downward." Saber held a straight finger on a slant to show the angle. "There was just enough force remaining to exit through his cheek. Once the swelling reduces we'll have a better idea of his condition. Nursing is what he needs most. In a couple of weeks . . ." He began putting his scarred medical bag in order and muttered, "He'll be back on the prod." Dr. Saber straightened and raised quarrelsome eyes. "His kind you patch so someone can kill him. They ride high for a time but all get buried just as deep. Too bad, in Tibbs' case. He's more of a man than most." The doctor closed his mouth with a click that matched the snap of his case and walked out.

Sid turned to Peggy Smith with a brusk question. "Ain't you one of Newt Gobal's girls? How come he let you nurse the marshal?"

"The judge arranged that," she answered, then added with a trace of annoyance, "And I'm *not* one of Newt Gobal's girls! I serve drinks and entertain the customers." She eyed him steadily. "And, Mr. Peel, that's *all* I do."

Peel's eyes narrowed. "You tellin' me the judge and Newt Gobal are that close?"

Her smile held mystery. "I only arrived in Pineville a few days ago. How could I possibly know how close anyone is to anyone else? I only work for Newt Gobal. Now, why don't you leave so this room can be a bit quieter?"

Nodding slowly, Sid turned toward the door then whirled back, with sudden resolve, to face Peggy Smith. She had leaned down to straighten the blanket and raised her head, waiting for him to speak.

"Can you do something for me?" Sid asked.

She was still suspicious and answered with a tart evasion. "That all depends on what it is."

"When the marshal comes around—you know, when he can talk and all, will you send someone up to the construction job and let me know?"

Peggy looked shocked. "Are you leaving him here all alone?" she demanded.

"You're here." He sensed something was bothering her—that she was afraid for the marshal. "What can I do here?"

"Everything is so mixed up," she countered. "I can't really say what it is. But, this marshal . . ." She shook her bright head, half in sorrow and half in pride. "This Marshal Orion Tibbs," she went on haltingly, "keeps coming back. Judge Yontz has given him a dozen chances to escape—to run off. Why doesn't he? He's not really a lawman. Why does he stay?"

"I don't know," the scout said uncertainly, but he had the same feeling about this woman as he had about the disreputable Dr. Saber. Both the doctor and this saloon girl were fighting for Tibbs' safety. The girl was motioning to the still form on the bed.

"Now—like this—he can't protect himself."

"But the judge . . ." Sid began, then recalled his distrust, his feeling that Yontz was in pretty deep in some devious manner. Could he leave Tibbs defenseless in the judge's hands? He watched the girl's face clear as he suddenly agreed to her unspoken request. "I'll stick around. Right now I've got a job to do at the cemetery." He smiled grimly. "Something else our sleepin' friend started. Afterward, I'll be back." She was smiling openly when he left.

CHAPTER FIFTEEN

During the following week, while Orion Tibbs floated in and out of a coma and Sid Peel patrolled the hallway with a cocked rifle, the future of the railroad was debated.

Roger Allan, bedeviled by his board of directors, had arrived at the construction site to inspect the tunnel damage and had arranged a meeting in Pineville's Palace Hotel. Allan and Judge Yontz wheedled and threatened interested parties to attend and explore the possibilities for bringing the railroad into Pineville.

Three members of the board, with authority to make a decision, arrived on the third day following the explosion. A night stage brought the grim-faced men into the Palace. After a few minutes of desultory talk and limp handshakes, they promised a full-scale hearing for the morning and withdrew to bed.

Judge Yontz and Roger Allan adjourned to Yontz's room. The engineer was grim as he faced Yontz. "Where was all that protection you talked about?" he demanded, cutting off the judge's protest by raising his voice. "I laid my career on the line. Who will ever hire an engineer who drove two hundred miles of rail up a mountain only to have it end in a deadfall? What can we expect to haul east of Crater Pass? Firewood for our engine? Apache mothers going visiting?"

"It can't be all that bad," Yontz offered, raising a mollifying hand. "Can't those tracks be brought in some other way?"

"Sure, on a five-mile trestle—built up from a two-thousand-foot foundation, in a canyon carrying torrents of snow water every spring!"

"If that's what it takes, that's what you have to do," Judge Yontz growled. He stared into Allan's discouraged face and raged. "Now you listen to me! Nobody ever walked away from a problem and licked it. We've got to convince that board of directors the trestle will serve. Then you build that trestle!"

"How? Paint it on the wall?" Roger Allan cooled a bit. "Who'd be able to protect the job? They blew up the tunnel; they'll blow up the trestle! They just don't want the railroad to come through the mountains. Garfield and Newt Gobal must be in this together. Tibbs might be able to protect us, but he's wounded and . . ."

"You want that railroad to run off into the desert?" the judge asked. "A one-stop terminal? Can you compete with Kansas and the North, just hauling cattle? Your market is the mines, the sheepmen and cattlemen. Coming west, you'll be hauling settlers, people who farm and buy what a railroad hauls, canned goods, barbed wire, blasting powder, and people who ship out hides, ore and timber. History will prove . . ."

"Save it for the meeting!" Roger Allan snapped.

"They'll listen, but you'll need more than emotional appeal. They don't care about history—they want profits *today*. Hauling cattle is profitable, especially when track-laying is cheap. They know the cattlemen are willing to subsidize the railroad and even give them the land to build on!" The engineer stalked to the door and turned to fire a parting salvo. "Gobal's in command. Any history will show it was the fortress of the badman, a sanctuary for every two-legged wolf . . ." he was still muttering as he slammed the door behind him. The boards of the balcony shook under the stamp of his feet as he turned to take the stairs.

The black muzzle of Sid Peel's rifle poked out of the dark and buried the barrel in Allan's stomach. "What's this?" He halted abruptly.

"It's the racket, Mister." Sid Peel's eyes were cold in the dim light. "The marshal's hurt bad and he's sleepin'. We don't want so much noise."

"You working for Tibbs?" Allan snarled, then subdued his anger. "How is Tibbs? Reports were that he was pretty badly mauled."

"He'll come through," answered Peel, moving close and lowering his voice. "You countin' on that judge to swing the meetin'?"

Sadly, Allan shook his head. "Nothing will change the directors' minds. Switching the track out of the mountains into Rail Head is logical; it's the only way they can salvage their investment."

"That so?"

"Something else?" Allan asked with asperity.

"Judge Yontz," Peel stated with conviction. "I'm

sayin' you better not trust such a secretive man too far."

"Bosh!" Allan snorted and pushed past the scout.

The meeting convened at ten in the morning. Newt Gobal had moved some ornate furniture out of the long lobby and replaced the space with straight back chairs from the poker tables. He had set up a dais for the three railroad directors so they could face the gathering.

Judge Yontz led the directors in and when the three men were seated behind the small table, the judge stepped forward and addressed the assembly. "These men seated here at the dais are directors of the company which is, at present, putting in the Territorial Shortline Railroad. They have cordially agreed that the citizens of the area should be heard as to the future of the railroad. Mr. Wolfstein, Mr. Simpson and, of course, Mr. Adams.

"Before Mr. Wolfstein addresses you, I wish to present some of the interested people." He pointed to the tight group of ten men seated to the right. "Our cattle-raising contingent. Mr. Piper Garfield will, no doubt, act as their spokesman. Next, on the opposite side of the room, is the owner of this establishment, Mr. Newt Gobal, and a few other townsfolk. Below the dais, in the front row, is our Omar Clay. Mr. Clay is Pineville's blacksmith and livery man. He also buries our dead." Smiling thinly, the judge turned back to the dais and addressed the railroad directors. "Mr. Wolfstein, would you like to make a statement?

Wolfstein parted his graying mustache and rose. Heavily, he moved back from the table and lumbered to the front. "Gentlemen, it was good of you all to be present. Of course, we can re-hash events for hours—such as why the tunnel was blasted or the advantages of continuing or discontinuing the line into Pineville, but this would be a waste of time. We're in the practical business of building a railroad. At this instant, we're basically interested in salvaging our investment. To do so, we must retreat . . ."

"Aye!" Piper Garfield interrupted. "The offer made by the cattleman's organization still stands. Run your tracks across the flatland into Rail Head, and we'll not only give you free right-of-way over our lands, we'll provide full protection."

"Yes, yes," Wolfstein said. "That's the kernel, the meat of the nut—protection. Without it, we are forced to abandon our mountain route. The Territorial Governor," Wolfstein threw a fierce scowl at Judge Yontz, "when we requested an Army detail, advised us we would only receive civil protection; that the Army was needed on the border. We were assured by Judge Yontz that the U.S. Marshal could handle any problems. This assurance was not supported. As you know, the marshal did capture the men who blew the Crater Pass Tunnel but only after the tunnel was blasted away. Our engineers tell us," he directed an arm toward Roger Allan, "the cost of trestling would be excessive. So, thanking you for your attention, we will hold a short caucus and report our decision." Wolfstein stepped toward the door and Simpson and Adams rose to follow.

"Just one minute!" Omar Clay was on his feet, his face pinched with fury, his lionlike head drawn down against massive shoulders. "*This* is what you call an open discussion? Our cattlemen spoke. Newt supports the cattlemen so he's sitting on his hands. Judge Yontz slumps like a busted waterbag with the spunk run out of him. But there's another side to this picture! Upstairs, Orion Tibbs, Marshal, lies in a coma. Therefore, I feel it's up to me to state some facts, so just give me your attention!"

Wolfstein, with studied reluctance, returned to the table and sat down. Omar began softly. "I'll not bore you with the advantages of continuing the railroad through the Tooloons. That's been right all along. I'm sayin' that running the tracks through the flatland won't stop all your trouble. Like the blast at Crater Pass, they'll be more trouble because you ain't got the men who's causin' all this trouble!"

"Eh?" Wolfstein perked up, and Omar gripped the back of his chair as he plunged on. "*I'm* sayin'—the blasting of the tunnel was engineered by Newt Gobal!"

"You're sayin' too damned much!" Newt Gobal was on his feet. A pair of his men slipped quickly to the back of the room, waiting. Judge Yontz waved off Gobal with a shout. "Omar has the floor, let him speak!"

"Not when he's accusin' me of . . ." Newt had almost reached Omar. The judge, on his feet, was trying to step between the pair but Newt pushed him off while Omar defiantly went on.

"Gobal," he shouted, "paid Yolo to blast that tunnel—everybody knows that. The railroad should have him arrested and . . ."

"You crazy son-of-a- . . ." Newt began but his raging voice was lost in the explosion of a rapid-fire Colt.

Startled men, feeling trapped in a room where the next slug might seek out an innocent bystander, broke for the exits. Judge Yontz recovered and moved toward Omar Clay. The big blacksmith, a stunned look on his face, was swaying. Newt Gobal had halted and was stepping back from the dying man. Omar reached out for Newt, lost his balance, and crashed to the floor. Yontz kneeled and rolled Omar onto his back, seeking vainly for a pulse. Sadly, he stared up at Newt.

"Is he *dead?*" Wolfstein had left the dais and was squatting beside Yontz.

Newt started to storm. "The bullet came through his back! I was standing right in front of him. I never drawed no gun!"

Wolfstein ignored Newt Gobal. "Who was this Yolo?" he asked Judge Yontz.

"One of the tunnel blasters," the judge replied.

Wolfstein, still hunkered, was studying the angular lines of Omar's dead face. "New Englander . . ." he muttered, then slowly straightened. "What a waste!" His face reddened with anger and he edged his stubby body up against Newt Gobal. The hotel owner, eyes suddenly veiled, tried to lean away but Wolfstein kept crowding forward. "Did this Yolo fellow work for you, Mr. Gobal?" he demanded.

"Not at all! He hung around here while he was in town but that's the limit of it." Gobal tried to glower. "I—I run a saloon. It's open to everyone!"

"Who shot that man?" Wolfstein pressed.

Jeering, Newt Gobal turned to the judge. "Take this—tycoon—take him out and explain. Who knows who shot Clay—or why? Maybe he owed someone and this someone used the excitement to kill him. Or," he glowered, "someone did it to make it look bad for me!" Newt turned abruptly and walked off.

Wolfstein spoke to the judge. "That series of shots came from the back of the room. When Mr. Gobal rushed forward to attack Mr. Clay, I saw two men hurry to the rear and stand there, as though waiting for a signal. *I* believe they were waiting for such a signal from Mr. Gobal."

Judge Yontz was still visibly shaken. "Are the men still in this room?"

Wolfstein shook his head. "It seems that I'll require more information." His tone was threatening as he indicated Simpson and Adams. "Can we go somewhere and talk in private?"

Yontz nodded quickly. "We'll cross over to the marshal's office. It'll be safe there."

Wolfstein nodded and explained. "Before Mr. Clay was murdered our decision was to abandon the mountain route. We were interested solely in the cost." He shook his head sadly. "Now we must become involved. This fight has brought death and destruction but we'll stick! If there is any other possible route, we'll bring our railroad through these mountains!"

CHAPTER SIXTEEN

The cold-blooded murder of Omar Clay startled Pineville. Concerned citizens gathered in the back street behind the cantina to argue a proper course of retaliation. Most agreed they had surrendered their town to the headstrong Newt Gobal and his hotheaded drifters. They had expected Judge Yontz to plug the breech of law and order—a single shield between safety and anarchy. Yontz had tried. When the Territorial Governor refused him Army troops, he had brought in Orion Tibbs to out-gun the madcap adventurers who terrorized the West and were now gathered in this northern territory. Pineville was becoming recognized as the capital of outlaw country. Now the failure of the railroad to conquer the Tooloons would assure lawbreakers of a safe hideaway.

The townspeople, with some pride, further admitted Orion Tibbs had also tried. He had gunned down Gobal's appointed lawman and had put the town on notice that a real lawman was in charge. When Newt had retaliated and called together a "kangaroo court," Tibbs was backed up by Omar Clay and Calaway. Now both were dead. Tibbs himself had suffered a debilitating wound and was now out of action.

What law, they asked themselves, remained? Only a stubborn but faltering judge and perhaps the scout, Sid Peel, who patrolled the Palace Hotel floors with a rifle to protect the wounded marshal.

"We need the cavalry!" Bill Haskins, proprietor of Haskins' Hardware and Feed Store, spoke out. He had joined the group behind Raphael's Cantina. When the men began to drift apart, Haskins made his pronouncement in a loud voice. "I know Yontz asked for troops," he added recklessly, "but he was brushed off because the troops are needed to patrol the border. Apaches are raiding, up from Mexico. The governor figures this is most important. 'Cepting now, since the railroad's been blasted to a halt, Omar killed and the marshal wounded, the governor should look at the other side of the coin. Newt's made this an oasis for every outlaw in the territory! We should *demand* troops and the governor'd better get them in here!"

"They could be a month on the way," a querulous voice spoke. "What will happen until they arrive?"

"Head for the storm cellars!" another laughed hollowly.

"Muster up a vigilante posse," snarled Bill Haskins. "Then we order Newt Gobal and his men to leave Pineville!"

"An' he shoves your face in a creosote bush!" taunted a tall copper miner. "You ever noticed how many men he's got? They're a-comin' and a-goin', 'specially lately. The last couple weeks, since Tibbs put that whole bunch in jail, the Palace reminds you of Quantrill's headquarters. I betcha he can raise five hundred men in forty-eight hours and . . ."

"On top of that, Yontz would be right on your back. He's for law and order and keepin' things legal," interrupted another. "And Newt's got this town blanketed—*that* you'd better believe! You get talkin' vigilantes in Pineville and you'd better bolt down that storm cellar."

Bill Haskins watched the knot of grumbling men break up. Shoulders drooping, he wandered up Main Street toward his store. As he neared the center of town, he noticed the lighted marshal's office and crossed the street. With loud resentment he banged on the heavy door. Judge Yontz pulled it open and, after a furtive survey of the empty street, asked Haskins to enter.

The three railroad directors lounged in the small office. Wolfstein's face was grim as Yontz made introductions. Simpson and Adams leaned back in their chairs. Simpson whittled off a bite of pungent chewing tobacco and offered the plug to the storekeeper.

"This meeting was about ready to break up," Yontz said, then added, "unless you have any suggestions on keeping this end of the territory alive. The railroad can't get through unless . . ."

"Unless we get Army protection," Haskins interpolated.

"Or hire Pinkertons," Wolfstein offered. "But Good Lord, what a five-mile trestle would cost!"

"There's no other route in all these mountains?" Haskins asked.

"We've been all over that," Yontz explained. "The Apaches have a moccasin high-road and the Spanish brought wagon trains through the Tooloons for a hundred years. . . ." He paused and Wolfstein broke in.

"It seems no one knows where those passes are. Our engineer, Roger Allan . . ."

"What's an engineer know?" Haskins was too angry to listen. "Go find yourself an old Indian scout or a man who rode the hoot-owl trail or a trapper. They'd take you through country your Boston engineer's never heard of."

Wolfstein showed interest. "There's such a man?"

Haskins shrugged. "Guess most of them are dead— or workin' for Newt." He brightened. "There's one other who just might be. . . . But hell, he's wounded!"

"Tibbs?" Yontz's face lighted with hope and he turned to Wolfstein. "Haskins could be right. Tibbs was high-riding this country for five years before he was jailed. He should know every ravine."

"How bad is he wounded?" asked Wolfstein.

"Oh, he's tough. In another week he might be on his feet."

"Here's what we'll do. We can delay a week." Wolfstein threw a covert look at his companions and when they nodded, he continued. "When Tibbs gets better . . ."

Simpson rose to his feet, a dejected stoop to his thin frame. "Another week in this place? Remember, we're carrying a mighty big payroll." The protest was made with humor, but the words held the quiver of a man fond of money.

Wolfstein smiled at Simpson's dejection. "Might just make better men of us all, to spend a week in hell!" He nodded around the room as he rose to leave. "We'll get on back to the hotel. See you in the morning."

Judge Yontz followed them to the door to bid them goodnight. When he turned back, Bill Haskins was still standing in the middle of the room. The storekeeper's face was set, his tone nettled. "Judge," he began, "I saw Holloran shoot Omar Clay in the back! More'n that, I'll swear I seen Newt give Holloran the high-sign!"

"You'd be perjuring yourself, Bill."

"We'd be rid of Gobal!"

"Would we?" The judge's bile was rising. "And who would arrest Gobal? He has an *Army*."

"So does the Territorial Governor!" snapped Haskins. Yontz fidgeted with some papers on Tibbs' desk while Haskins went on. "There's something mighty big going on. Why is the governor giving this whole country to Newt Gobal and his kind? In a week the troops could scatter this rat's nest, but they're held down on the border. Tibbs is wounded. It's like Newt Gobal's *testing* the governor. Daring him to . . ." Haskins broke off, eyes narrowing over the puzzle. "Say, Judge, do *you* know what'n hell is going on?"

"What're you talking about?" Yontz evaded.

Haskins suddenly had a knowing look in his eyes

and the bit in his teeth. "My wagons . . ." he started slowly. "I've been shipping supplies south of the mountains. Rifle ammunition, saddle gear—even barley and oats. Sacks of beans and slabs of bacon. There're twenty men camped at Buffalo Creek, another fifteen at Devil's Slide, where the Apaches were slaughtered. There're fifteen men out there in those rocks . . . What for? Say, Judge, I'll bet we've been supplying maybe two hundred men!"

"And you think they're Gobal's men?" Yontz asked with a crooked smile.

"It all goes on Gobal's account!" A mixture of amazement and cupidity pinched Haskins' mouth. "But what for?"

"Who knows?" the judge answered nonchalantly, moving quickly away from the desk to lower the wall lamp. With his free hand he waved the storekeeper out and blew across the rim of the chimney. Outside, the judge stepped off toward the Palace. He turned and threw a brief goodnight to Haskins.

Haskins wasn't finished and he shouted after the judge, "Those men were on guard! They're posted there to fight off the Army! Does Newt Gobal want to fight the whole Army? What the hell, Judge!" Haskins spat into the dust. "When we catch up with Newt, this whole country'll go back to the Indians."

The judge, reaching the hotel steps, whirled to answer, reconsidered and muttered to himself, "What's he want from me—miracles?"

Peggy Smith, from a vantage point at the window in Orion's sick room, had watched the railroad directors leave the marshal's office. She waited until the light went out and turned back. The candle stub had burned down but it caught the marshal's face and glinted against his open eyes.

"Peeking, Peggy?" The words were raspy and weak.

She crossed the room and reached for a comforter. He caught her hand. With a patient smile she tugged but he held on. The white gauze patch over his cheek raised to show he was smiling.

"You startled me," she said. "At least it looks like you've decided to come alive."

"What's out there?" he persisted. "You were as tense as a calf on a rope."

"The judge was meeting with the railroad directors . . ." she began, then clucked softly. "But you don't know about that, do you?"

"Depends. I suppose they came in about the tunnel blasting?" He looked up into her anxious face and added gruffly, "Something more has happened?"

"Something more," she said and withdrew her hand, stepping back from the bed before telling him about the meeting in the hotel and the sudden murder of Omar Clay. Peggy Smith concluded with a somewhat frantic appeal in her voice. "They'll come for you next. Only Sid Peel has kept you from being killed."

"Sid Peel?" His voice cracked with remorse over the killing of the jovial liveryman. "What's Sid doing here?"

"He found you," she explained. "Your prisoner,

Cash, was dead. You'd been shot but you reached the road. Don't you remember?"

"Getting shot, yes. Not much else. Why—why was Omar killed?"

"He challenged Newt. Not only that—they wanted him killed. It was like blowing up the tunnel and robbing the stage. They're up to something very big and very dangerous. We're trying to find out . . ." She raised her hand to her mouth and began to talk rapidly. "The judge and the railroad directors were meeting, then Bill Haskins went in and . . ."

"*Un momento,* senorita," Orion cut her off. "Go back a bit. You said—'we're trying to find out.' What does that mean?" He waited, then chided, "Who are 'we' and what are 'we' trying to find out?"

"Oh, everyone," she equivocated. "Newt seems to want the troops sent in." She crossed the room and blew out the candle. "But we've talked too much. You go back to sleep. The judge will want to talk to you in the morning."

"I hope he makes more sense than you do," grumbled Orion. As she closed the door, he noted his holstered gun still hung from the bottom bedpost.

CHAPTER SEVENTEEN

Orion Tibbs tried to stay awake and think through what Peggy had told him. He had been in a coma. Several days must have passed since he and Sid Peel had outgunned Yolo and his three partners. Sid Peel's presence could be accounted for. The scout had brought him in, then decided to stay around to forestall any attack by Newt Gobal's crew. The railroad officials Peggy had named would naturally meet. According to Roger Allan's fears, they would decide to pull the tracks out of the mountains and relocate their line so it would cross the flat desert country and terminate at Rail Head.

Omar's killing was a genuine shock. The genial blacksmith had been a man and Orion knew he owed him. That was one debt he intended to pay off. After this he would quit this crazy U.S. Marshal masquerade, collect the hidden stage payroll and kite out for Mexico. The money had been laying dormant too long, yet each attempt he'd made to gather it in had been frustrated. Calaway's death, the tunnel blasting —even Yontz's constant harangues about law and order had kept him lying around Pineville. But what had Peggy Smith meant . . . ? Orion gave up and dozed off.

The clean crack of a rifle shot, followed by the

click of an ejected cartridge, brought Orion wide awake. Daylight glowed against the faded green window shades and tinted the yellowed wallpaper. Following the gunfire, feet shuffled down the outside balcony and halted at Orion's door. He raised himself, and felt the sharp shock of his wound. Holding on to the bedpost until he recovered, he gingerly swung his legs onto the floor and reached his holster. The metal was warm and comfortable but its weight sagged in his weakened hand. He was trying to balance on wobbly legs when the door eased open.

Behind a smoking rifle barrel, Sid Peel's deepset, hawkish eyes stared in. When Peel located the gun in Orion's hand, he smiled. "Came alive, eh? Smell of powder? Bugle call to a war horse?" He stepped across the room to press Orion back onto the bed.

"Something going on?" Orion asked.

Belying his levity, the scout's hand caressed the rifle breech and his lean neck was tense as he answered, "In time, but first I've been wrong about a man and will take a minute of your time to honor him." Orion settled back, waiting. Peel went on.

"Doc Saber . . ." He stated the name reverently. "He has lived with a sullied reputation too long. The man was his own self-elected judge. He only allowed those he disliked to die. The proof? One U.S. Marshal with an exploded head, is still alive because of the skill of the deceased, Doc Saber."

"Deceased?" Orion was perplexed.

"Can you make it to the window?" Sid Peel led the way. With the rifle barrel, he flipped the curtain and stared warily out. Reassured, he nodded for Orion to join him.

A handful of men, hampered by the hitching rack and the watering trough in front of Haskins' store, were raising the body of Dr. Saber. The familiar black coat was dripping water and the thin hair had fallen over the doctor's face.

Orion's mind went back to the night of the "kangaroo court." Dr. Saber's testimony and that of Art Peaker had supported the contention that Roddy Ryan had been shot in the back. The doctor had lied and supported Newt Gobal, right down the line. Why then had he saved the same man his own testimony might have hung? Professional pride? Or had something ignited the spark of manhood self-abuse had withered away?

Watching the limp form unceremoniously dumped on the rough boards of the walk, Orion felt rage supplement his own frustration. "Who shot him?" he demanded.

"Newt done that killin' himself," Sid Peel answered softly. "The doc took a chance and tried to stop them from kidnapping the railroad directors. Newt just opened up and plugged the old fella."

"They kidnapped the directors?" Orion asked. "Why?"

" 'Spect 'cause Newt figured it was time to move out. Anyway, every man Newt's hired—and that's most every gunslinger in the territory—rode out a few minutes ago. They took Wolfstein, Simpson, and Adams along.

"That's stupid!" snapped Orion. "Men like that, building a railroad, have powerful backing. The governor will have troops headed this way in very short order."

"Yeah, maybe you're right," answered the scout.

"We'd better find the judge." Orion withdrew from the window and began slipping into his clothes. Remembering, he turned back to ask, "You fired a shot?"

"A fellow started up the back way," Sid replied blandly. "I flung him a warnin'. You know, Newt Gobal don't like you none, either." He stepped back to let Orion stagger through the doorway. They hurried along the balcony and rapped on Judge Yontz's door.

"Who's out there?" Yontz's voice was muffled.

"Me and Marshal Tibbs," Peel growled. "Open up, Judge!"

The door swung open on creaking hinges; twin barrels of a shotgun appeared around its edge. "Step in and walk straight ahead!" Yontz snapped.

"Don't be stupid, Judge." Orion found his voice. He walked in and turned up the wick of the lamp. As the glow lighted the room, Judge Yontz moved away from the door to lean his shotgun against the wall.

"I thought you were flat on your back," he said peevishly.

"I was, Judge." Orion smiled at Peel. "I was until this galoot started shooting." He turned serious. "Newt Gobal's gone and taken the railroad directors with him

The judge's face was solemn as he tried to bring the whole picture into focus for the marshal. "You've been out. Peggy tells me you did a bit of raving but never really knew where you were, or what happened."

"She finally explained that last night," stated Orion.

"Then we'll go into what happened this morning," the judge said. "Those three—particularly Wolfstein —seemed mighty determined to bring their railroad over the mountains, like it was planned. Neither Newt Gobal nor Piper Garfield liked that idea, but Wolfstein's got a mind of his own and he was staying on in Pineville until you came out of your coma."

"What could I do about the railroad troubles?" Orion was puzzled.

"Your name was brought up, Orion. Haskins figured you'd know these mountains pretty good. They were your hideout territory for the best part of five years, so he figured you might show them another route, a lost pass or something." He paused, but Orion remained silent. Yontz went on. "Anyway, they stayed on in Pineville so they could talk to you. Then early this morning, Newt Gobal went and kidnapped all three of them."

"And murdered Doc Saber," reminded Sid Peel.

"In cold blood," added Yontz. "Just as they did Omar Clay when he accused Newt of blasting the tunnel."

"But a deliberate killing and a kidnapping! Newt

must know he'll never get away with it. Every law-man in the territory will . . ."

"Don't be too sure. When the stakes are high enough, some men will attempt the impossible and bring it off." Yontz's statement was brittle and flavored with caustic. "Newt Gobal's been building his army for a long time. He's . . ."

"Army?" Orion interrupted. "If he's got an army, so have we. Bring the soldiers in from the border."

Yontz cut him off with a shake of the head. "That's exactly what he wants us to do." He held up a palm to complete his statement. "Let me explain. This was only headquarters for Newt. You never saw one-tenth of his gang. Only the leaders reported in. The rest are camped out all across the territory. From Ashfork to Gallup, and on to the Santa Maria Mountains and Walnut Canyon. Twenty men in one place, thirty in another. Three hundred—maybe five hundred—all waiting for the big raid."

"The big raid?" Orion Tibbs stole a look at Sid Peel's noncommittal face. "We heard about that in prison. A clean sweep of the territory. Every town bank, cattle herd, supply depot, and even the mines were to be hit. One big scoop by a thousand men and an escape to interior Mexico. Most of the cons figured it was another pipe dream."

"No pipe dream," Yontz was positive. "And Newt Gobal's the chief. It's his scheme."

"But why would he want to bring the troops north?" Orion, still shaky from his wound and half-

bewildered by the series of atrocities committed in
the last few hours, was beginning to feel a deepening
anger. Why hadn't Yontz leveled before, told him
about Newt's army of gunfighters? Without waiting
for the Judge's answer, he exploded. "You've been
rousting me! Holding back and . . ."

Shaking his head, Yontz tried to calm the marshal.
"I was planning on explaining, Orion, but you got
shot and before that . . ." He spread his palms, his
words drifting off.

"Before that *what?*" bellowed Orion, then had to
raise a hand to his aching head. "Before that . . ."
His own voice drained out and the room was silent.
Why should the judge have given him his full confi-
dence? Orion grimaced as he thought back. Hadn't
he cached the payroll? Hadn't he intended to shake
Calaway, recover the money, and ride off to Mexico?
Even at the railroad gunfight, he had subconciously
intended to drift away. Of course the judge wouldn't
have had actual knowledge of his convict-marshal's
intentions, yet the judge was shrewd and played his
hunches. Numbly, Orion faced the judge. "I—I guess
you didn't really trust me." His words sounded hol-
low but had to be brought out.

"From the time," Judge Yontz spoke slowly, choosing his words, "you lost the payroll. How could I
trust you? Emma Clay was the only one left alive. She
said you were gone some time and she heard gunfire
—three rifle shots. Yet you told her the two bandits
got away. Mighty poor, Orion—you getting in rifle-
shot range and letting them simply ride off."

"The woman," Orion mumbled defensively, "was there alone with night coming on. Lord knows what could have happened to her . . ."

"Sure, sure," Yontz said calmly. "If you say they rode off with the payroll, then they rode off. I'll believe you now, but I didn't then!" He dismissed the subject and asked, "What can we do about catching up to Newt before he kills those railroad men?"

"First thing to do is to start after them!"

"Not a'tall," was the surprising rejoinder. "First off, you're not able to ride hard; secondly, that's just what Newt expects us to do. More'n that, even, he wants us to raise a big fuss with the governor to get troops up here." He moved restively around the room, deep in thought. Orion looked at the silent Sid Peel. The scout made a wry face to denote his own puzzlement and shrugged.

"I can ride," snorted Orion. "Of course, if you want to let Newt get away with it and butcher those three railroad tycoons . . ."

"Sit down." Yontz laid a friendly hand on Orion's shoulder and led him to a chair. "Have a glass of whiskey. Sid, can you find Peggy Smith and bring her around here?" As Sid Peel left the room, the judge softly added, "You see? Peggy's with our side."

"Our side?" Orion flushed. What could the judge mean? He had seen Peggy sneaking into the judge's room but thought . . .

"Wait until Peggy gets here, Orion," Yontz said, then added with a cryptic glance at Orion's guilty face, "We must've fooled *you*, at least."

CHAPTER EIGHTEEN

Newt Gobal, astride a white stallion, raised a gloved hand to halt his band of fifty men. Coming up ahead was the narrow defile of Crater Pass. Lights flickered high on the shelf above the bowl where men, still searching for buried bodies, toiled through the night.

The moon, low in the west, was half-hidden by scudding clouds which shadowed the heavy face of the bandit chief. His eyes, hard and bright, caught the moonlight and ignited the savage power he exercised. He leaned back to rest one hand on the rump of his restive animal and called over his shoulder, "Bring up that smallest one—the one called Simpson."

Simpson was brought forward and Newt reached out to yank the kerchief from the man's mouth. "You can stay alive," he shouted, "but them two"—he waved toward the dark blot that enclosed Wolfstein and Adams—"them two are going to die mighty hard if you try anything funny. Understand?"

Simpson fidgeted. His arms, drawn tightly behind, secured by a rope laced between his elbows, were numb. He had already seen Newt Gobal shoot down Dr. Saber and knew this belligerent man wasn't bluffing. He managed a nod of assent.

"Let loose his dally string," Newt ordered, and Simpson felt the rawhide rope loosen. "You get up there." Newt pointed. "They got a telegraph so you report to the governor. You tell him to pull his troops off the border. If he does that, we'll let them other two free when we reach Mexico! If he *don't* do like I say, we'll have to string 'em up!" Newt glowered for a few seconds. "Think you can remember all that?" Simpson nodded and Newt slapped the rump of the small man's lathered horse and hooted as it galloped toward the construction building.

"Tommy!" Gobal shouted to a slight man wearing a white hide vest. "Tommy, you skirt around to the west of the tunnel. Soon as you figure Simpson's sent his message, you cut the telegraph wires. After, you follow us along the tracks and every couple of miles, cut them again. Savvy?" With a terse nod, the man swung his horse off the road and the white vest faded into the night.

"There, let's say the big raid is damn well started!" Newt muttered and swung off the saddle. He walked back to the riders and motioned another man to dismount and follow. The pair walked a full hundred paces off the road and halted. "Curley, you're my ace in the hole."

Curley spat and dug two fingers into a shirt pocket for Bull Durham. "Them two railroad galoots'll make pretty good insurance."

"Some," agreed Newt, "but in a big raid like this, we got to have more insurance. We gotta ram at least one hundred thousand cattle down the chute, right into Chihuahua. We've gotta rob every bank, store, and mine in southern Arizona and haul the loot across the border with us. Now, let's look at all the angles. The payoff's been arranged. Political strings all unraveled. Only one thing left to do . . . S'all, only one small detail . . ."

"Sounds good so far," Curley accepted the statement.

"That one small thing," Newt continued, "is to get the Army off the border. If they block the chute at Pozo Verde . . ." he shook his head, "we could lose the cattle and . . ."

"But if they come north after them two railroad tycoons, that'll sure leave the crossin' at Pozo Verde open for us!"

"Maybe, Curley." Newt's mouth tightened and he stared into the dark. "But maybe ain't good enough, so I figured somethin' else. Kidnappin' them directors was done—well, on the spur of the moment 'cause they just happened to be around. They was handy, see? With a big raid, especially with three hundred men, there's got to be some leaks. Now, Yontz knows somethin' and he's passing it on to the governor. That's why them troops're still on the border."

"What could Yontz know?" Curley was skeptical. "Tibbs, maybe, but . . ."

"Don't you forget," Newt was thinking out loud, being very patient, "we been plannin' for bettern'n two years and some's been caught and locked up. A place like Territorial Prison, full of men—they gotta talk. They got a grapevine, so Tibbs has got to know something about the raid. 'Course he don't know it all, just like the judge don't know it all. I figure they got a good idea we're going across the border at Pozo Verde. Two or three hundred blue-bellied troopers stationed along there could wipe us out."

"Kind of late to be worryin' about that now," grumbled Curley.

"*Now?*" Newt straightened and glowered down at his associate. "Jackass in a trundle bed! I been tryin' to get them soldiers north for better'n two months. Knocking off stages, rustling Garfield's cows, stealing horses, and even conductin' a 'kangaroo court!' When Yontz brought in Tibbs for U.S. Marshal I figured Roddy Ryan could kill him, but he couldn't. I had Tibbs picked up and was going to give him a 'kangaroo court' lynchin' and that didn't come off. I even tried to get a war going between us and Garfield, but Tibbs stampeded Garfield's herd and that blew up. That damned Yontz just won't ask the governor for the troops!" His face darkened. "Blowin' up the tunnel was next and still Yontz wouldn't move. And I don't think he'll get very excited about askin' for the Army to rescue three railroad directors. All this time," Newt yanked a twig of greasewood out of the ground and began to draw a map in the sand, "we've been cooling our heels. Winter's going to hit pretty quick. We've got to get on our way . . ."

"Sure we do." Curley watched Newt's twig tracing lines in the sand. "But if them troops ain't comin'?"

"You're going to bring them!" Newt was pleased with his map and used the twig as a pointer. "We're here . . ." He drew an "X." "Territorial Prison is about here." He made another "X" and gouged a straight line between the two marks. "You take fifty men, get up to that prison, break into Yuma and get them prisoners out. That'll bring the troopers!"

"Sure will," Curley was pleased. "Breakin' *into* a prison is real different." Suddenly he frowned as the full implications of Newt's plot penetrated. He gave Newt a level look and made—for him—a long speech. "Say it works—this jailbreak. The troops come north when they learn there's fightin' at the prison. At forced march, even the cavalry will need a week. You could run head-on into them. What's the payoff if you don't get through with the cattle and the bank loot? We'll be fightin' all the way to Mexico and there's nothin' . . ."

"We won't run into the soldiers because we'll be up in the Tooloons." Newt was excited now and jabbing the stick into the ground to make his point. "When the troops go by, we wait maybe two days longer. By that time they arrive at the prison, but you get the prisoners out. They've got guns from the prison arsenal and'll give the soldiers a hell of a battle. You fight a delaying action, drifting south. That leaves nothing except a few lawmen and cowboys between us and the border. We'll shove the cattle right along and take any town we figure's worth looting. You just hold them one week—just one week—then cut for the border. How's that sound, Curley?"

Curley was doubtful. "You think you can push cattle twenty miles a day? They gotta be rounded up and . . ."

Newt Gobal smiled and broke in. "The ranchers don't know it yet, but I got men workin' on every range. Some hired on and others're laying out in camps, all ready to start shovin' the herds south. They got orders to cut down anybody who tries to stop them." Newt was stalking around, slashing at the chaparral bushes as he talked, then came to a halt in front of Curley and demanded. "You got any more dam'fool questions?"

Slowly Curley shook his head, his expression indicating admiration for Newt's sagacity. "I'll get the men and we'll cut out north right now."

Newt hit his companion a hearty slap on the back. "Atta boy!" he boomed and threw away the stick. "You get the best job, Curley. Givin' them bluebellies hell!"

Curley nodded and followed his chief back to the horsemen.

Meanwhile, in the judge's room at the Palace, Orion and Sid Peel straddled a pair of straight chairs and listened to Peggy Smith. Judge Yontz was seated on the narrow windowsill as Peggy paced about, talking.

"The judge had me paroled from the women's jail in Phoenix . . ."

"Like me!" Orion's startled exclamation slipped out.

"Like you, Orion." The judge was smiling as he raised his feet and hooked a heel on the sill. "Go on, Peggy."

"So I've been working undercover," she added defiantly with a faint trace of shame. "And gradually I learned something of Newt's big plan. His entire gang, including those who came in, and those still hidden out in his camps totals about three hundred members. He intends to sweep every loose dollar, every cow in southern Arizona, right into Mexico. Once there, the money will be divided, the cattle held or moved east to Matamoroa and sold in the Eastern states. Or they can be moved West and brought across into California. Newt's been making payoffs in Mexico for over two years. He knows once across the border he'll be safe."

Orion nodded. A dollar in Mexico went an awfully long way, but he didn't dwell long on that aspect. Peggy's revelation that she'd been working for the judge suddenly answered a lot of questions. He admitted his feeling of distrust toward the judge could have been the result of his suspicions about Peggy's clandestine meetings with Judge Yontz.

"We had to do it this way," offered the judge, as though reading Orion's mind. "Everyone around here must've thought I . . ." He blushed and Peggy giggled.

"Never mind, Judge," she said sweetly, "the other girls think you're quite a catch!"

"Well, Marshal," the judge became brusk, "what's Newt's chances of pulling it off?"

"You've been on this a long time," Orion countered, "so you must've thought he could get away with it."

"I certainly did. And I convinced the governor that Newt was fired up enough to go through with it. That's why he took such extraordinary action in letting me have you and Peggy paroled. And it's also the reason he's holding the Federal troops on the border." Yontz's tone was a combination of worry and pride.

"Then Gobal must figure the governor will change," guessed Orion. "When he hears of the three railroad directors being kidnapped, Newt could be figuring the governor'll send in troops."

"The governor agreed," Yontz barked, "not to move a single soldier off the border until I asked him to!"

"Then Newt may kill all three of those men," Orion said, and everyone in the room turned and watched the judge's face grow ashen.

He dropped his eyes but his jaw was rigid as he replied.

"Better that three men risk dying than a hundred be sacrificed. Once Gobal starts moving, they'll kill anyone in their way. I'm betting he won't move so long as the troops stay put. By pulling in the troops, we may be signing a death warrant for the three men he's holding."

"Are you sayin' you think Newt'd let a beautiful scheme like that just peter out?" Sid Peel's tone was horrified.

"No," admitted Yontz. "Not just peter out. They may make a raid here and there—a bank or a stage. But no amount of men could shove a herd of cattle across Arizona into Mexico as long as those soldiers stay put. A few cattle, yes, but nothing worthwhile and . . ."

"I know Newt Gobal's not going to sit in these mountains with three hostages until the snow flies," Orion interrupted, and saw Sid Peel nod. "I think we'd better track him. What we'll be able to do once we locate him, we'll have to decide then. " He looked around the room and saw Sid nod again. The judge scowled, slapped his knee impatiently, then moved away from the window.

"We can't do anything else," the judge admitted. "But another thing—we've got to get up to the construction camp and use the telegraph. The governor's got to know Newt Gobal has opened the game."

CHAPTER NINETEEN

The sun came up slowly over the highest of the Tooloon peaks. Clouds were thickening, changing from a washed cotton to a powder-streaked gray. A rising wind whipped the slopes, brushing the larger trees and slapping at the chaparral.

Peggy Smith, bundled in an Apache blanket and a pair of sheepskin squaw boots, sat on the high seat of the mudwagon and guided the team. Sid Peel, rifle resting on his saddlehorn, walked his horse a half-mile ahead of the wagon. Orion Tibbs slumped on the rear seat and tried to forget his pounding head. Judge Yontz, back braced against the driver's seat, snored fitfully. Mick and the judge's riding horse, both saddled, were on a halter rope behind the wagon. They appeared a pathetic crew, three men— one wounded—and a girl, setting out to frustrate Newt Gobal's long-planned dream of conquest.

Orion stared out past the canvas curtain. They had left Pineville during the night. In a few hours they would enter the familiar Crater Pass. Out here, in this dry rolling country, they might well be in another world. The wind blew, sand crunched beneath the wheels and, except for the ruts of the road, there wasn't a single sign of habitation. Yet Orion knew that hidden in the trees above and trailing over the

steep crags, Newt Gobal led his gang. When he cap-
tured the railroad directors, Newt Gobal had cut his
string. He had continuously flouted the law in Pineville, waltzing his tricky dance just inside the
boundary, and had taken all he could grab without
getting burned. Now he was an admitted outlaw.
Like a Juggernaut, his army was on the move, and
before it ground to a halt or reached the haven of
Mexico many men would die. Orion gave a fatalistic
shrug. A girl driving a wagon with two lawmen; a
railroad scout up ahead; this minority on the trail of
the largest bandit gang ever assembled in the West. A
gang with the most to gain and . . .

"Sid's riding back!" Peggy called out.

Orion and the sleepy judge looked up. The scout's
horse was galloping and Sid rode low, his body as one
with the animal. The tassels on his jacket were flailed
by the wind, the front brim pressed back against the
pointed peak of his hat.

"Rein in the horses!" Orion snapped at Peggy and
clawed his rifle off the creaking floor. When Peggy
pulled violently on the reins, the sudden stop threw
Orion off balance and the momentum carried him in
a shaky leap to the ground. The shock of his landing
sent sparks behind his aching eyes and he staggered.
Yontz clambered down.

"What the hell?" he demanded querulously.

"Sid's run onto something." Orion levered a cartridge into the gun's chamber.

"Look—up there!" Sid Peel was pointing as he slid

off the horse. "Look past that first ravine—higher up along the mesa. See?"

Orion, staring, saw horsemen heading north. The long line, obviously unaware they had been spotted, threaded through the trees growing beneath the mesa lip. Orion whistled softly.

"Better'n fifty men," Sid stated. "Suspect that's at least half of what Newt left out of Pineville with."

"But why north?" Yontz demanded. Consternation and awe shaded his words. "Why north?" he gulped. "The action, and all information, indicated the raid was to take place south of the Tooloons!"

"There's not a damned thing up that way." Sid Peel was equally puzzled. "Garfield's herd is being moved south, grazin'. What can fifty men be wanting . . . ?"

Orion leaned back against the wagon bed and continued to stare. Newt Gobal was smart. To put life in a raid that would cover most of the territory . . . That could be it—Territorial Prison!

"What *is* that crazy Gobal up to?" Yontz moaned, then brightened. "You don't suppose they're leaving? Some sort of row?"

Orion caught Sid's crooked smile and shook his head as he hunkered down against the wheel and motioned the others forward. "It's Newt's way of forcing the governor to send his soldiers," he said quietly. "Newt's sending a party north to raid the Territorial Prison!"

Hope shattered on Yontz's face as the truth of

Orion's statement penetrated, but he fought the thought. "That's just a wild guess!" he shouted.

Peggy Smith was staring wide-eyed and Sid Peel answered Orion with a wry nod of agreement. "It's more than a guess," Orion said calmly. "The prisoners know something about the 'Big Raid.' There were plenty of grapevine guesses. Warden Lowdnes and Carl Clopper were both mighty nervous. Some men tried to escape to join the raid. Every man in that prison would give his right arm to break out. From here, it looks like Newt's going to give them a chance. Fifty armed men can capture that prison!"

The judge slumped, accepting Orion's evaluation but anguished by the failure of his plan to capture Newt at the border. Now he would have to warn the governor and have the troops hurried North. Yontz groaned as he pictured Newt's hordes slashing South, gleaning everything valuable, including thousands of prime cattle. Newt had won. The border would be wide open. Dimly, Yontz heard the marshal's calm voice and began to listen.

". . . and we send Sid north."

"Sid? North?"

"Damn it, Judge, listen! I said, Sid will try and beat the gang to the prison. One man on a fast horse —especially Sid—can outride fifty men. He warns Warden Lowdnes. They'll have a chance to fortify and hold out until the troops get there."

"But that's the trouble!" wailed the judge. "The troops'll have to be called off the border."

"No, no," Orion's voice was still slow and calm.

"We'll get the troops from Fort Defiance, up north of here. The governor can send *them* to protect the prison. Newt's communications are going to get pretty bad. About all he can do now is pass out orders to his lieutenants. He'll have some cut out all the cattle south of Frazier Wells and drive for the border. Another gang hits the banks and loots the towns, like Williams, Prescott, Wickenburg, and so on. You see, the territory is so big he can't change much, because each unit will be miles from the others. Once he's moving . . ."

Yontz interrupted vehemently. "I see! So he'll think the troops from Fort Defiance are those who're still protecting the border?"

"Of course, Judge. That's been his big hurdle. Now he's sending those men north to open the prison. He's only thinking south of here, plotting to get the border open. My guess is he's told these men to break out the prisoners, start south, and hold the Army back for a week. Rear guard action. Delaying tactics are easy. Every canyon becomes a fort. A few men can hold . . ."

"I understand all that." Slowly, Yontz repeated Orion's words. "Newt won't know the troops are from Fort Defiance. He'll begin moving south—into a trap at the border." Suddenly he flailed his arms in frustration. "What I've been trying to say—there's only three of us! Someone has to get to the governor . . ."

"And we've got to think of Peggy," Orion said.

"You're not sending me back!" She objected with

such vehemence the restive horses started and she yanked back on the reins, lowering her voice. "I've put up with the hassling around at the Palace Hotel, I've been sneered at by half the girls and hated by the other half. Most of what you know about Newt's plan I discovered in that pesthole of a saloon! Don't you dare think—now that everything's becoming settled —I'm going back to Pineville and sit on a down couch while three men try to stop HELL from taking over the Arizona Territory!"

Orion Tibbs grimaced and threw a protective hand to his forehead as he caught Peggy's stormy eyes. She blushed and decided not to continue her tirade, but smiled faintly and shot him a pleading look asking for support.

He gave it grudgingly. "The judge had better head out for the construction camp and use their telegraph. He can get through to the governor and any orders he sends can be on the Army telegraph to Fort Defiance. Peggy can go with the judge." Her quick smile was his thanks and Orion swiftly continued. "Sid will ride hard for Yuma Prison. I'll ride out on Newt's trail. I can at least keep track of Newt and maybe get those railroad directors."

"We'll have Newt Gobal in a pincers," Yontz started to gloat. He climbed into the seat next to Peggy, waited until Orion freed Mick's lead rope, then shouted, "Get this team going, girl!" She kicked off the foot brake and cracked the whip. The team sprang forward. One wheel skittered over a flat rock and the mudwagon swayed, corrected, then lined out for Crater Pass.

Sid Peel circled behind his pony and leaped into the saddle with a smooth vault. He watched the wagon crashing along the ruts for a few seconds and addressed the marshal. "You know what you're gettin' into?" Without waiting for Orion's reply, he let out a yell and lashed his pony on a dead run toward Yuma. Orion watched as the scout turned once to wave. He waved back and gathered in Mick's reins.

"I wonder," Orion muttered, "if he meant a battle with Newt Gobal, or getting friendly with Peggy?" He mounted and eased Mick into the chaparral. Well, a man had to think of a woman sometime in his life!

The most important thing to think about right now was Newt Gobal. The quick decisions necessary to stop the big raid had sounded fine, but implementing those decisions was another task. There were so many possibilities which might spell failure. Delay, for one. The governor had to be convinced to send the cavalry unit from far-off Fort Defiance. Orion didn't doubt Judge Yontz's ability to convince the governor that the success of the entire plan depended on keeping the border troops on post. And, what if Newt's men defeated the cavalry at Yuma? Would the governor still hold tight? Those border troops *had* to be there when Newt's gang tried to funnel the cattle across the border. Unhindered, Gobal's scourge could sweep through Arizona. Law officers were few and scattered in the thousands of square miles of the territory. Newt's crafty deployment of his gang units could wipe out the law like a kid switching heads off cattails.

There was only one real chance to prevent the carnage that would occur if Newt got his plot into operation. Inwardly, Orion smiled at Peggy's words; hell *would* settle in the territory and the devil would fill his graveyards. Newt Gobal would have to be cut down—not when he reached the border, but before the bandit's plans could be put into full motion. It is hard to stop the sweep of a scythe in the middle of the swing and there was only one way to stop Newt's swing. Orion decided he would have to catch up to Newt Gobal and put a slug into him. And that, reasoned Orion Tibbs, thinking back over the death of Omar Clay, would indeed be a pleasure. Mick, sensing the mood of his rider, gathered his chunky body together and broke into a gallop.

CHAPTER TWENTY

Hours later, Orion rode up the underlip of the mesa. He dismounted, pushed aside the low branches of a pine snag and searched until he located the tracks of Curley's men. Orion whistled in the grazing horse, remounted, and began to backtrack the trail.

With the sun only hours from setting and splashing on Mick's withers, he broke out on top of the mesa and cantered forward. Boulders and shallow ravines spaced the uneven terrain to slow his progress, but Orion knew that up ahead Newt Gobal and his crew would be drifting south. At dusk he reached the spot where Newt and Curley had held their powwow. Curley's tracks to the north now mingled with a larger party. Orion guessed that at least a hundred men now rode with Newt. Somewhere ahead they would make camp. Newt would have to hold back and delay, perhaps several days, to allow Curley time to reach Territorial Prison, start his fight, and suck the border troops forward.

Now that he was sure of Newt's direction, Orion dropped off the mesa into Cold Ravine. This was familiar country to the marshal—renegade country. He had hidden out in these windswept canyons for many months; he'd trapped and prospected to while away time until the law wearied and dropped off his trail.

Orion followed Cold Ravine a dozen miles past the rim of the mesa before daylight disappeared completely and he was forced to make camp. Beyond the precipice of pure lava, Cold Ravine sloped into swampy Grass Lake. The runoff from Cold Ravine was dammed against the solid lava flow. The water gathered behind this natural dam and, in the late summer heat, stagnated. A few hundred rods beyond the massive embankment, Roger Allan's railroad roadbed passed on its steep climb to Crater Pass.

Orion found a dry spot under an overhanging ledge, gathered green branches and bullrushes for a bed and made a cold camp. Mick nibbled at the short grass bordering the stream but Orion Tibbs went hungry. At dawn he was again on his way, hoping to cross the right of way unseen, and then continue on over the next ridge into the higher Tooloons. This should put him in front of Newt Gobal. Somewhere out there in those familiar crags and wooded slopes, he would catch Newt in his rifle sight and hot lead would put an end to this big raid.

By eight in the morning he reached the right of way. A work train chugged by, leaving the cut. The engineer ducked when he spotted Orion and poured on the steam. The engine dropped out of sight quickly and Orion crossed the tracks. On the far side he inspected the telegraph line. The cut wire sagged between the poles. He felt like cursing. This could only mean that Judge Yontz had failed to reach the governor and the prison would be overrun in short order. Even with Sid Peel's warning, the few guards couldn't expect to hold off fifty of Gobal's professionals. Newt would soon have five hundred more recruits happy to join his big raid. With his own following swelled by the prisoners, Newt Gobal could give the troops at the border a good battle and break through.

Recklessly, Orion urged Mick forward. Newt's camp would have to be found quickly. Orion's hopes of rescuing the kidnapped men and gunning down Newt Gobal would have to be delayed. Someone from the railroad crew would have to carry a message to the governor, or better yet, Roger Allan could dispatch a light engine down the mountains where the telegraph contact could be made with the governor.

A hard hour's ride brought Orion out of a shade-splashed canyon onto a high ridge. Directly below lay a large camp. Newt Gobal, still brashly confident that everything was going his way, had made his main camp only five miles beyond the railroad right-of-way. He had chosen a hunting camp used by the Apache. Several *hogan*-type cabins squatted beneath rocks that towered along a canyon wall. A rope corral, straddling open ground that contained a seeping spring, held a remuda of churning horses. Several men lazed near a cave opening and watched steam curl up from the large cooking pots. Meat, spitted above open fires, wafted a delicious smell upward.

Orion dismounted and crept forward. He reached a spot fifty yards from the overhang and studied the camp. One of the rock cabins was guarded by a pair

of riflemen. Obviously, Wolfstein and his partners
were still alive and being held prisoners in this make-
shift jail. Washed vari-colored shirts and socks, were
draped Mexican-style over stubby bushes to dry. A
man had a small fire compacted between rocks to
gain enough heat to fit horseshoes. Orion felt better.
This camp looked like the men had settled in for a
stay.

From his vantage point, Orion scanned the camp
limits until he could pick out the guards. One sat a
horse at the narrower end with his attention directed
south. At the higher end, two men were seated with
their backs to the bank, staring out at the ridges
which sloped up from distant flatlands. Orion bit his
lip. Not a single man patrolled along the back trail.
It didn't make sense . . . The neck hairs rose on his
neck. Someone in back of him had exhaled a deep
breath. He rolled away and had his Colt out when he
reached his knees.

Two men with rifles cocked faced the marshal's
Colt. One was Judge Yontz. His eyes, riveted on the
gun barrel, were bulging, his mouth fallen open. Finally, he found his voice. "Hold on, Orion!"

The marshal took pressure off the trigger and exhaled sharply. "Where'd you come from?"

Yontz motioned forward his companion, an Indian. His black hat, decorated with a yellow-tipped
feather, was pulled down over long, braided hair.
Yontz's voice was still shaky. "This is Fish-hunter,
with the railroad crew. He's Apache and led us up to
this old Indian summer camp."

"Us . . . ?" Orion asked with kindling hope.

"The engine man saw you," explained Yontz, "when you crossed the tracks. He reported, so we figured you'd found Newt's trail. Roger Allan's got forty tracklayers and they're all loaded for bear. Right there—beyond the last rise. Fish-hunter and me," he added proudly, "tracked you this far, and Fish-hunter says the camp is just beyond."

Orion nodded. "About a hundred yards." Quickly, he explained the layout of Newt Gobal's camp. "With forty men and some blasting powder, plus the element of surprise, we can get at Newt and end this big raid before it really gets started."

"We've got to do something fast," the judge admitted glumly. "The telegraph wires are down."

Orion nodded and still hunched, led Yontz and the Indian guide away from the overhang. He found a low spot protected by rocks and halted. "Judge, you get on back to the engine. Race it down into the flatlands until you can find a place where the telegraph is still working. Get your messages sent. The governor will still have to send troops from Fort Defiance to protect Territorial Prison, but he can free his border troops . . ."

"I don't buy that part!" Yontz snapped. "Even with Newt out of it, there's plenty others already rounding up cattle and . . ."

"And killing will start at the first bank they hit!" finished Orion. "The governor will have to divide his soldiers and send out a squad to every town with a bank. Alert every lawman; every constable, sheriff, and U.S. Marshal. With soldiers *and* lawmen, the raiders will run into more gunfire than they can stand."

"And the cattle?" Yontz was still unconvinced.

"It takes time to move cattle," answered Orion. "Without the help of Newt's main body, the ranchers can fight off the raiders. That make sense?" Slowly, Yontz nodded.

Satisfied, Orion sent Fish-hunter back up to keep watch on the raider's hideout, then led Judge Yontz back to the right-of-way. The judge, with a wave, boarded the engine and Orion watched it descend the grade.

Orion located Roger Allan. The engineer was leaning moodily over the railing of a flatcar, staring at the disappearing engine. "Yontz tells me your men are ready for some fighting?" Orion asked, moving up the steps to stand beside Roger Allan.

"They've got a mad on," admitted Allan. "Newt Gobal did more than kill the tunnel miners, he ruined a damned good railroad. A lot of these men will be out of work . . ." He paused and gave Orion a sardonic look. "But those are my troubles, so you just show my gandy dancers where Newt Gobal's raiders are holed up and they'll chew them to pieces!"

"Fair enough," Orion said. "We'll hold back until dark. Planting a few charges of explosives in the right places and a controlled rifle fire should finish up Newt Gobal. Can you have the men put together about two dozen medium charges, strong enough to blow down shale rock? Then make sure they all have rifles and plenty of ammunition?"

Roger Allan nodded and stepped off the flatcar. In a short time, he wandered back and grunted. "They'll be ready in short order. You've located Gobal's camp?" At Orion's nod, Allan asked, "Wolfstein and . . . ?"

"Safe so far. And while we're waiting . . ." Orion pointed to the crag rising straight up from the right-of-way. "Did you know that's a plug of lava?"

"The Tooloons," wryly answered the engineer, "is a prehistoric taffy pull. Bedrock pressed to the surface, and lava caps seamed with shale ledges . . ."

"Behind that plug," Orion interrupted, "is Grass Lake. Beyond Grass Lake, Cold Ravine slopes easily up the east mesa."

"So . . . ?" Roger Allan was giving Orion avid attention, hope rising in his eyes. "The east mesa at Pineville?"

"The mesa east of Pineville," Orion said.

"This Grass Lake," Allan was fascinated. "How deep?"

"It's a swamp. Maybe waist-deep, right now." Orion grinned at the engineer. "What do you think?"

"We could tunnel through the lava plug," chortled Roger Allan. "Drain off the swamp. With an easy grade to the top of the east mesa, we could drop right into Pineville."

"You think your directors will go along?"

"Let's get them out of Newt Gobal's hands and find out."

Orion studied the sun. Long scaling shadows had begun to cover the rocky face of the cut. The breeze he'd noted the previous afternoon was again gathering strength. He whirled with a sudden thought to ask the startled Roger Allan, "Say, what happened to Peggy?"

A faint smile gathered around the engineer's lips. "Nothing's happened to her." The smile grew into a chuckle. "But she sure was ready to boil us all in oil! She's back at the construction camp and mad as a hatter." He winked. "She said that if we didn't find you, the judge and I had better get lost!"

Orion grinned, then turned solemn again. "Let me have your notebook." When the surprised Roger handed it over, Orion Tibbs drew a hurried map of his Wells Fargo payroll cache. He pressed hard to make a firm X where they would find the treasure box under the shale. With the feeling that Carl Clopper was already re-opening the cell door, Orion passed back the notebook. "If you'll follow this map, you'll locate the stolen railroad payroll." He stepped away and changed the subject.

"By the time we get the men into Newt's camp, it'll just about be dark enough."

CHAPTER TWENTY-ONE

Fish-hunter's teeth glowed in the darkness. He laid a calm hand on Orion's elbow to lead him back a few steps. One of Newt's guards, a fresh knife-cut through his yellow vest, lay face down in a cul-de-sac of boulders and tall grass.

"They sent out guard maybe short time ago," explained the scout. "One dead fella, already. We no need worry about surprise. Pretty good, eh?"

Orion gave Fish-hunter a grateful nod and turned to wave the crew of railroad workers forward. Fifty feet from the rock overhang he motioned them down. At his silent nod, Roger Allan crept forward. "There are the three *hogans*. Your people are in the center one. See how it's guarded?" He pointed, and Allan nodded.

A rifleman hunched alongside the narrow door. Below, a good fifty yards farther on, was the horse lot. A stack of hay, fenced in with cut brush, blocked one end of the corral. "Newt's headquarters," he said coolly, "are in the next *hogan*—the one nearest the bank. Most of Newt's men are under the ledge, camped out of the wind. Tell your powder gangs to ease up to the overhang. The men with rifles will lay back. The first explosions will be enough to roust the men out from under the ledge. Once in the open, the rifles can cut them down. We'll be above them and in the dark. When the explosions start . . ."

Roger Allan objected. "It's pretty dark for effective shooting."

"We'll be fixing that." Orion nodded to Fishhunter. "We'll sneak across to the horse lot, touch off the haystack, and cut the picket ropes. The haystack should light up the camp and give plenty of targets. Before they can recover—that's when you hurry in and release the prisoners. Hightail them back up this way. Savvy?" At Allan's nod, Orion ordered, "Then send your powder gangs into action and let's begin this war!"

Roger hesitated. "What about Newt Gobal?"

The marshal turned grim; his voice was cold. "*I'll handle Newt.*"

Orion followed the Indian over the ledge and they dropped the twenty feet onto the shelf holding Newt's camp. The dark peaks behind threw a heavy shadow over the lower level. It was the time of evening when hunger made men restless and small groups were drifting toward the cookwagon. Orion and the Apache, keeping to the deeper shadows along the overhang, began working their way around the edge of the camp. A hostler, tossing hay to the cavvy, turned and grumbled, "Time some help showed up. Grab a pitchfork an' start throwin' hay." He halted and stared suspiciously as Orion kept moving forward. "*Not* there . . ." he began, but the rest of his sentence died forever under the lean edge of Fishhunter's knife.

Even as the man fell, Orion joined Fish-hunter and began wrapping barley sacks into the tines of a pitch-fork. Seconds later, they lighted the sacks and raced around the haystack. The fire, licking at loose straw, started slowly. Long moments passed while the pair hurried back to the corral and slashed away at the taut picket ropes. The animals, startled by the sud-den flames and keening yelps, reared away from the dangling halter ropes. In seconds, the mass of rampaging horses tore the corral apart. Higher up, surprised men began to shout and run toward the dis-turbance.

Orion tapped his partner and they dodged out of the light. The fire had gained the top of the stack and the heavy smoke, with the help of the wind, burst into red flame. The guard at Newt's *hogan* was on his feet and raising his rifle. Several heavy explosions erupted and he whirled back toward the bank. Men, outlined by the fire, hesitated, and the volley of rifle fire from Allan's men smashed across the camp and cut them down. Orion had one quick look and saw the guard go down. Without waiting, he and Fish-hunter ran toward Newt's headquarters.

As they arrived, the door popped open. Several men rushed to circle along the adobe walls, trying to locate the rifle fire raining from the overhang. Newt, buckling his gunbelt, reached the doorway and hesi-tated.

"Over here, Newt!" Orion shouted and watched the heavy frame pivot, glaring out. Orion raised his Colt and triggered one shot but Newt, recognizing

Orion's voice, had twisted away and was outside. He took three heavy strides and was gone behind the *hogan*.

Orion ran forward but heavy fire from the railroaders drove him off and he had to circle wide. He found a dark spot and lay on his stomach, waiting. In a few seconds Newt Gobal made his dash for escape, but was caught in the light from a haystack. Orion snapped another shot and knew he'd missed. Newt had again reached the safety of darkness. His heavy bootsteps carried him into a growth of buckbrush. Orion rose to his feet and followed the bandit chief. The ground was spongy from rotting leaves and Orion halted to listen. The railroader's guns still spat and the excited trumpeting of frightened horses carried into the brush.

A stick cracked and Orion, whirling, dove away from the sound. Newt's Colt exploded above Orion's head. He jerked away and fired upward. Slowly, Newt's Colt hand dropped and the heavy body swayed. Orion climbed to his feet as Newt crumpled. His body rolled a few feet and halted against the thick willow stalks.

Orion turned away and marched into the open. An eerie quiet greeted him. The haystack still blazed and wisps of burning hay drifted about the camp. The men behind Newt's *hogan* had crept back and now stood, hands raised, staring up at the overhang.

"Throw down all your weapons and move into the light!" Roger Allan shouted harshly. As Orion hurried ahead, the raiders were gathering in the open.

"Send out Newt Gobal!" added Allan, then again raised his voice. "Marshal? Are you all right, Marshal?"

"All right," Orion called back. "Newt Gobal is dead."

Orion leaned back against the railing outside Judge Yontz's room and watched Peggy Smith step from the hallway onto the balcony. The tiny worry wrinkles which had drawn her slender brows together since the fight at the Apache camp had lifted. Yontz realized that Peggy, underneath a poise of studied indifference, had also worn those wrinkles of concern since Judge Yontz had left for Tucson, over a month ago.

The night of the attack on Newt's camp, Yontz had gotten through to the governor quickly. Newt's telegraph cutters had stayed above the flatlands. Beyond, on the sandy flat, the telegraph had been operative. The governor had gotten the Fort Defiance cavalry moving and they had arrived at Territorial Prison on the second day of Curley's siege. Sid Peel had done his job well, alerting Warden Lowndes' defenses, and they had managed to hold out until the arrival of the Fort Defiance soldiers.

On the southern end, at Pozo Verde, Newt's big raid had gotten fairly well underway. His flatland raiders had begun moving the cattle south. Again, the governor had acted swiftly by alerting lawmen and moving border troops north. When Orion and Roger Allan had, with the help of the forty railroad-

ers, overrun Newt's main camp, the big raid had
drawn to a sporadic halt. Some of the men had escaped into Mexico; others, with vengeful marshals
hard on their trail, had scattered into the badlands.
Wanted posters with heavy rewards were already out
and the bounty hunters—men who trapped human
animals for gold—were also in pursuit.

The "Big Raid," long the wildest dream of bad-
men from Kansas to California, had at long last been
tried, only to fail. Newt Gobal had pulled most of the
fine target hairs together but had missed the mark.

Roger Allan's railroad, via the Cold Ravine route,
would be entering Pineville the following spring.
Allan would go on to bigger engineering tasks, but
he would never forget the night he helped destroy
Newt Gobal's dream of conquest.

"Sid rode in." Peggy had reached the small table
and settled into a rattan chair. Orion nodded. "He
said the judge is on the stage."

"Oh?" Orion answered softly. "Then I expect we'll
be hearing pretty quick."

"Pretty quick, Orion," she said, and rocked slowly.
Then in a quick burst of feeling, added, "Whatever
the decision, Orion, I want you to know I don't
blame you one little bit."

"That's nice to know, Peggy," he said thoughtfully. "I never realized, or rather never understood
the advantage of being a *real* lawman." He flushed,
but continued. "A man could have a—a home—with
a wife and family."

Her bright head was lowered and he could see the

part in the shining hair, which was braided and knotted with a yellow ribbon contrasting against the faint gold of her skin.

"Have you ever thought about that, Peggy?" he asked.

She lifted her face and nodded. Excitement glowed in the blue eyes and a hint of mischief threaded her reply. "I've thought about it more times than you have, Mr. Orion Tibbs!"

"Then—then you will?" He stepped forward, hesitated, and slowly drew back to his original position.

"Will I what?" she asked pertly. Noticing his retreat, her tone was suddenly gentle. "If everything goes wrong, Orion, even if the judge . . ."

"If the judge—what?" Leander Yontz was advancing down the balcony, his boots whacking against the boards. He drew up in front of the pair and waited for his answer.

Orion took the bait. Clenching his teeth he leaned forward and gritted. "Don't roust me, Yontz! Get down to it. What the hell did you and the governor decide?"

Judge Yontz teetered back on his heels, cast an owlish look at Peggy, and twisted his mouth into a wry smile. "It wasn't really decided in Tucson."

"No?" Orion spat out the word, glanced at Peggy and choked back his anger.

"The governor was tough. He took convincing," Yontz said. "Finally, he put it this way. 'Yontz,' he said, 'you go on back to Pineville. You left this fellow Tibbs on his own. Now, if Tibbs hasn't skedaddled, you tell him . . .'" Yontz held up a hand to halt Peggy's exclamation. "'You tell him that as long as the railroad got the payroll—eventually—the charge of robbing a stage will be dropped. You also tell him he's pardoned for all past crimes. He'll be expected to stay on as U.S. Marshal. . . .'" Judge Yontz grinned, made a smart about-face, and strode quickly off.

Peggy crept close to Orion Tibbs, who circled her warm shoulder with a firm arm. She raised her face and he kissed her.